ABOUT THIS BOOK

At his cousin's pleading, Karson Kane returns to Havenwood Falls to help with his elven uncle, who's about to be released from supernatural prison. Karson has no idea what awaits him in the mysterious mountain town, but he feels strongly he's meant to go.

Within the first twenty-four hours, Karson's cousin gets thrown in jail, too, and Karson ends up in the ER, leaving him to think he may have made a mistake coming to the magical town. Until he meets Scottlin Glover. The gorgeous, auburn-haired breath of fresh air treats his injuries, but leaves him wanting more from her, as he can't seem to take his eyes off her.

Scottlin is very intrigued by the elven. Being only half human, she has ways to both heal and help, but she can't figure out how to help Karson when they realize there's something terribly wrong with him beyond the initial injury.

Karson begins to suspect that he has been lured to Havenwood Falls under false pretenses, but can't seem to find any answers. If he and Scottlin can't put their scorching attraction aside and heal Karson, the consequences will be more serious than they imagined—and very permanent.

HAVENWOOD FALLS BOOKS

Forever Loyal by E.J. Fechenda

Fate's Demand by Emily Cyr

The Wu & the Wand by T.V. Hahn

A Demon's Redemption by JD Nelson

Also try the YA line, Havenwood Falls High; the historical paranormal line, Legends of Havenwood Falls; the darker, sexier side of town, Havenwood Falls Sin & Silk; and the local supernatural college, Sun & Moon Academy.

Stay up to date at www.HavenwoodFalls.com

BOOKS BY C.J. PINARD

Paranormal Fantasy:
Enchanted Immortals 1
Enchanted Immortals 2: The Vortex
Enchanted Immortals 3: The Vampyre
Enchanted Immortals 4: The Vixen
BSI: Bureau of Supernatural Investigation
Enchanted Immortals Box Set: 4 Books + Novella

New Adult Contemporary Romance:
Patriotic Duty (Duty & Desire, #1)
Tour of Duty (Duty & Desire #2)
Boots Beneath My Bed (Duty & Desire #3)
Playing the Field (Duty & Desire #4)

Romantic Suspense:
Antihero (Imperfect Heroes, Book 1)
Above Protection (Imperfect Heroes, Book 2)
Beneath Broken (Imperfect Heroes, Book 3)
Beyond Love (Imperfect Heroes, Book 4)

Paranormal Romance:
Unscathed (A paranormal romance novel with Tim O'Rourke)

Soul Rebel (Death's Kiss #1)
Soul Redemption (Death's Kiss #2)
Soul Release (Death's Kiss #3)
Kovah: Soul Seeker (A Death's Kiss Novel #4)

Lotus (Daughter of Darkness) Lotus's Journey Part I
Watcher (Daughter of Darkness) Lotus's Journey, Part II
Guardian (Daughter of Darkness) Lotus's Journey, Part III

The Lunar Effect (The Ayla St. John Chronicles, #1)
The Lunar Curse (The Ayla St. John Chronicles, #2)
The Lunar Secret (The Ayla St. John Chronicles, #3)
The Lunar Magic (The Ayla St. John Chronicles, #4)

Reverse Harem Fantasy:
Four Princes (Rothhaven Trilogy, #1)
Four Kings (Rothhaven Trilogy, #2)
Four Heirs (Rothhaven Trilogy, #3)

AFFLICTION MINE

A HAVENWOOD FALLS NOVELLA

C.J. PINARD

This is for all the Havenwood Falls authors. Thank you so much for sharing your characters with me—with us. You've created a world I want to live in.

CHAPTER 1

KARSON

*T*he backpack was getting heavy, and I shifted it to my other shoulder as I wondered just where the hell this Greyhound bus was. It was supposed to depart at 10:20 a.m., but as of yet, it wasn't even here in the station.

"Karson! Hey, dude!"

I turned around and spotted my coworker, Dex, waving at me.

Oh, God, what does this guy want? I wondered as I watched him approach.

"Happy new year. Where you going, man?" he asked, staring at me as he took a swig from a black and green can.

"Going out of town. Why are you here?" I asked, keeping it vague so he'd go away.

"Same. Goin' to see family. You know." He shook his head before taking another swig of his caffeine-loaded drink as he measured me with a curious stare.

Seriously hoping this pothead wasn't on the same bus as me, I smiled tightly at him and said, "Great. Well, see you next week." I turned and headed toward the vending machines that lined the back of the Greyhound station.

Just as I was about to choose a bag of jalapeño-flavored potato chips, the loudspeaker announced that the bus to Montrose was leaving. I quickly shoved my dollar bill into the machine and willed the bag to drop so I could board the damn bus.

Once I snatched the chips from the bottom of the machine, I hustled to the boarding area, presented my ticket, and found a seat in the back, just wanting this stupid trip to be over with. I had other shit to attend to, and dealing with my "cousin" and his weird-ass request wasn't what I had on the agenda for the holidays.

Still . . . I literally couldn't remember when I had last been to Havenwood Falls. A part of me wondered why most of my childhood was absent from my memory, but I knew it had to do with the sleepy Colorado town. Had I really grown up there?

I pulled out my phone and clicked on the email app, deciding to re-read the cryptic message for the hundredth time.

Karson,

This is going to sound weird as hell, but hear me out. I need you to return to Havenwood Falls like, yesterday. I know you're thinking, "Return? When was I there?" Well, you have been here. You grew up here. You don't remember because the town is full of witches and other supes and shit. You leave, you don't get the luxury of remembering it at all. The witch bitches are gonna have my ass for telling you this, but I don't have any fucks left to give at this point, so here goes.

My pops, your uncle, is in a bad way. He used his affliction to piss off the Court and was sent to prison. Why am I telling you this? Because he's gotta do six weeks in jail here before they release him back to us. Before you ask why you should care, here's why: My dad's a loose cannon. In his late 40s and still ain't learned shit about shit. I need you to help me put a leash on him once he gets out. The Kane name has been muddied enough. Oh, and also, your dad is here (they're brothers), and he's been asking about you. It's getting old, and you need to come home. Of course, you prob don't remember your dad, but still.

Fuck . . . I know this email is so damn weird to you, but you have to trust me, cuz. Head up to Havenwood Falls, and you'll see. Once you get here, your memories will return. All of them. It'll take a hot minute, but I promise it'll happen. It's gonna be a trip, bro. Take a bus to Montrose, and when you get off, there will be a special bus to Havenwood Falls at the stop there. Hop on it, and don't ask any questions. I'll swing by and get you at the coffee shop, which is the last stop for the bus. We'll talk then. Reply with your itinerary, dude. I need you here pronto.

    Jalen

My head was spinning. The email had literally come out of nowhere yesterday, and the only reason I sat on this damn bus right now was pure, unadulterated curiosity. I hit reply on the email and told him I was on the bus heading to Montrose, but had no idea when I'd actually reach Havenwood Falls, as there was no online schedule to the place that I could find.

But the part of the email that touched on getting my memory back and the mention of my father had definitely sweetened the deal. As a twenty-four-year-old living on my own, I'd always taken care of number one. Nobody had ever been there to help me. I knew I had parents, but I could never get ahold of them. They never answered my texts or calls. I looked down at my phone and clicked the *Contacts* icon. Sure, I could click on *Dad*, but I knew it would go to a generic voicemail box.

It always did.

Hell, I couldn't even remember what my parents looked like or their names.

Then the email from this Jalen guy came in, promising me answers. It would have been a cold day in hell before I'd turn that down. I had no idea if he was shitting me or not, but hell, I'd take the chance. I had to. What did I have to lose, really? I was tired of wandering aimlessly, no matter how busy I was, always wondering if I had a family.

Half of me was hopeful this Jalen character was telling the truth and could fill in the missing pieces I felt had been absent from my brain. The other half of me was terrified that someone was playing a joke on me—that someone was running a hustle, and I would, yet again, be caught up in some shit I should have just walked away from. I had been lucky the guy hadn't pressed charges that night in the bar when I let my temper get the better of me over a stupid game of pool.

I pushed that from my mind and continued to click. I had to clear out my emails, because once I reached this mystery town, I knew I'd have no time for shit.

The next email to pop up on my phone was from a particularly needy client. Willing my eye to not twitch before I opened it, I took a deep breath and began to read:

Karson!

I want a Smurf. I need a Smurf! On my ass, or maybe my inner thigh ;) I know you can pull it off, can't you, cutie? ~Angel

I swallowed down my irritation and decided not to even reply. I deleted Angel's email and hoped she'd get the hint that I didn't want to tattoo her.

Ever.

A few weeks ago, she'd come into my shop in downtown Colorado Springs, tagging along with a friend. The friend was pleasant enough, just wanting a small tattoo of something to commemorate her father's passing. It was an easy tat, but what wasn't easy was the friend, Angel, who'd sat and stared at me as I worked. Sure, she'd pretended to be looking through the photo albums of my designs, but I knew she was checking me out. I could feel the weight of her stare as I tatted her friend.

When the friend's tattoo was done, she had been very happy with it, and paid me and thanked me profusely. Angel, though, asked me for my number. In deflection, I'd referred her to the front counter, where Dex would have given her a business card with the email address to our general box.

The crazy bitch used it, too. She'd sent me no less than six emails with photos of tattoos she wanted, and then suggested we meet up "in private" to talk about them.

Shouldn't I have been flattered? I guessed I should have. But at this time in my life, I didn't want to deal with such entanglements. Angel was hot, but I wasn't into pushy women. I was the one who called the shots.

I eventually drifted to sleep, and was awoken hours later when the bus driver indicated over the loudspeaker the stop we'd just reached: Montrose.

CHAPTER 2

KARSON

*T*he cold air hit me like a slap in the face as I hopped off the bus and looked around. A truck stop of some kind greeted me. There were gas pumps and a large, convenience-type store with a red and yellow logo.

Not seeing any buses marked Havenwood Falls, I adjusted my backpack and wandered into the store. I needed to take a piss, anyway. The restrooms were clearly marked, and after I used the facilities, I went to wander around the shop, wondering what I should do next. I was starving, so I bought a premade sandwich and a bottle of Mountain Dew, along with a bag of beef jerky. I spied a small sitting area, and made my way toward it to eat my dinner. The bus ride had taken twice as long as it would have if I'd driven, and I'd only had the chips.

On my way to the tables, I passed a rack of brochures boasting all Colorado had to offer for recreation and tourism. A brochure for Telluride caught my eye. Something about the way the mountains in the photo were positioned in a box canyon intrigued me. Flicking my gaze away from it to make sure I wouldn't run into anything as I walked, my plan was to set my food down and come back for it. But as my gaze shifted back to the brochure, I thought my eyes were playing tricks on me; for where I could swear it had read "Telluride," it now read "Havenwood Falls."

What in the hell?

Of course, I immediately snatched the pamphlet from its resting place and quickly made my way to the tables, never taking my eyes off it. I blindly unwrapped my sandwich and bit into it as I set the pamphlet down on the table and unfolded it. Its glossy photos called out to me. As I stared at it, a knowing feeling began to swirl in my gut. I'd seen that canyon before. Everything inside of me said I had been there before. I knew it deep down in my soul.

I opened the first page of the brochure, and my stomach began to turn over even more. Photos of familiar scenes seemed to jump off the page and smack me in the face. I knew that ski resort. I knew that inn. I knew those waterfalls. I knew that town square. And I most definitely knew that fucking tattoo shop.

My eyes scanned every inch of it, and when I flipped to the back, bright yellow writing caught my eye: *Buses to Havenwood Falls depart daily at 12 noon and 12 midnight.*

A glance at my watch showed 8:57 p.m.

Looked like I had three hours to kill, because come hell or high water, I would be on that bus.

After surfing the web, checking social media, and people-watching, a couple hours had passed, and I was getting anxious. I grabbed my bag, got up, and wandered over to the corner of the store.

I approached a store employee who was stocking coffee mugs bearing various Colorado logos and pictures. "Excuse me, can you tell me where the Havenwood Falls bus stops?"

She turned around, a mug in her hand. She dipped her eyebrows in confusion. "I'm sorry, I don't understand what you're asking me."

She seemed nice enough, but her response frustrated me. "Havenwood Falls—you have a bus departing at midnight. Does it meet out front? Is it marked?"

She shook her head. "I . . . I don't know where that is, so I can't help you. But maybe my manager knows. I can go get him—"

I pulled out the pamphlet and practically shoved it in her face. "See?"

She narrowed her eyes at it, then looked at me. With a shake of her head, she said, "That says Telluride. That bus meets out back. It's clearly marked."

I pulled the brochure back to my face to see it did, indeed, say Telluride on it.

What in the . . . ?

Feeling like I was going crazy, I checked my watch to see it was 11:51 p.m. I left the store and went around to the back, where a large bus depicting a mountain scene with *Havenwood Falls* written on it sat idling, no passengers on board, just one driver seated up front. I looked around to see if anyone else was in the parking lot, but it was deathly quiet.

I suddenly realized I didn't have a ticket, but I approached the bus anyway. The door was open, so I stepped inside and looked at the driver. He smiled at me with warm, brown eyes and waved me on, his face crinkling at the corners of his eyes. "Welcome!"

"Um, hi. Thanks. Where is this bus headed to?" I asked cautiously, remembering how the lady inside the truck stop couldn't see the brochure the same way I had.

"Well, where do you want to go?" he asked jovially, his pale skin looking almost sickly under the one orange light illuminating the parking lot.

Here goes nothing. "Havenwood Falls?"

"Well, you've come to the right place, elf. Choose a seat, and we'll be on our way!"

I blinked at him a few times before quickly checking my reflection in the large overhead mirror at the front of the bus. I was glad to see my glamour hadn't slipped, as the driver had given me a strange look. Sighing, I pushed a stray blond strand from my forehead and looked at him.

The old driver grinned at me and then looked down at the

newspaper he'd been reading. At that moment, the only thought I had was to exit the bus and just run. Hitchhike, Uber . . . something, and get the hell out of Montrose and go back to my mundane life. But something even stronger than fear was pulling at me to stay on that bus.

So without another glance at the driver, I took a seat in the middle of the bus, set my backpack on the seat next to me, and blew out a breath. To my surprise, the driver closed the door, put the bus in gear, and began to drive. I glanced at my phone to see it was midnight on the dot.

Feeling weird that I was the only passenger, but too tired to give a shit, I used my backpack as a makeshift pillow and quickly fell asleep.

The first thing I felt was cold. As I blinked my eyes open, I could see I was still seated on the bus, I was alone, and it was dark outside. The door was folded open, but the driver was gone. I wiped drool from the corner of my mouth and stretched.

After wearily grabbing my bag, I made my way down the aisle, and off the bus. As I stepped down, I could see I was in front of the coffee shop Jalen had told me about. The January air was chilly as hell, and I was only in a hoodie and jeans.

With my breath pluming out in front of me in foggy puffs, I hurried toward the shop and hoped it was still open. But judging by the darkness behind the windows, I wasn't optimistic. So I wasn't surprised when I tried to pull open the front door to Broastful Brew and it was locked up tight.

The hissing sound of air brakes caused me to turn my head. I saw the bus's doors close and its wheels turn, pulling away from the coffee shop.

"Shit," I murmured, wondering what I was going to do now.

What had I been thinking? I had hopped on this bus, without even waiting for a reply from Jalen, and now I was stuck, at two in the morning, in a strange town in the bitter Colorado winter cold.

I pulled my cell from my pocket, and—surprise, surprise—I had no cell service. "Awesome," I grumbled.

As I looked around, I could see I was on some kind of main street in the tiny town. There were tons of little shops lining the street. I saw a stoplight, a park, and briefly wondered where the alleys between the shops led to. With nothing else to do, I began to walk west, hoping the town also had some kind of motel nearby I could hole up in so I could regroup and figure out just what the hell I was doing in this godforsaken place.

What had I been thinking?

CHAPTER 3

KARSON

*I*gnoring the cold, I continued to walk down the dark streets of this strange town. But . . . was it so strange? I wasn't sure. There was an air of familiarity about it that I couldn't deny. I wasn't scared or stressed. In fact, I felt sort of at ease, despite not knowing where the hell I was or where I was gonna lay my head down for the rest of the night.

As I passed by a planter box set next to a tree, I saw it empty and sighed. I couldn't wait for springtime and all the flowers that would bloom once more.

I continued walking and lifted my gaze when I could see someone approaching. He was tall and imposing—and he wasn't alone. Two others flanked him, and they were walking right toward me on the sidewalk. I looked left, then right, wondering if I should just remove myself from this situation. But there was nowhere I could go.

As the three got closer, their white hair and pointed ears shone under the almost full moon, and I relaxed.

"Karson?" someone called out.

I stopped walking and adjusted my bag on my shoulder. "Jalen?"

"Damn," I heard him say under his breath. "Yes."

The three approached me quickly. They were definitely elven, with their pointed ears, pale skin, and white-blond hair. We could always sense each other.

Jalen put his fist out. "Sorry I wasn't at the coffee shop to get you. I wasn't expecting you."

I bumped it with my own, and said, "I replied to your email, like, hours ago."

He held up his phone, its bright light almost blinding me. "The cell service here sucks donkey balls, man. I went home and checked my emails on the laptop with the Wi-Fi and saw it just now."

What in the hell have I gotten myself into? I wondered. Shitty cell service wasn't going to work for me.

"Okay . . . well, I have a shitload of questions."

He laughed and shook his head. Shoving his hands into the pockets of his plain black hoodie, he said, "Like what?"

I flicked my gaze between him and his two compadres. "First off, who are they?"

"Oh. Damn. I forgot your memories are fucked. This is Tarron." He pointed to a beefy-looking dude who couldn't have been older than eighteen—and then he patted the other on the back. "And this is Gavin."

Gavin nodded, and I could sense he was the strong, silent type. He wore jeans and a denim and cotton jacket, and looked like he'd rather be at the dentist.

Tarron slightly jutted his chin at me in greeting. "What's up, cuz?"

I furrowed my brow in confusion, and put my attention back to Jalen. "You got a place I can crash?"

He grinned. "Of course."

As they started to walk, I followed. After a turn off the main street, we weaved our way down a few side streets. We finally found ourselves at the end of a cul-de-sac at a mundane-looking two-story house. Jalen opened the front door with a key, and we all followed him inside. It was a simple structure, average-looking, with nice living room furniture, a kitchen beyond that, and a steep staircase to the left.

"There are rooms upstairs. I'll show you yours," Jalen said as he began to climb the stairs.

Tarron, Gavin, and I followed him up. I felt this strange mix between apprehension, weirdness, and complete comfort stirring inside of me.

Jalen pointed to a closed door. "You can crash in there."

"Thank you," I said.

But as soon as I touched the doorknob, something flashed in my brain. I fell to my knees, a pain like no other searing my head, and everything went black.

She took a long drag from her cigarette, the smoke smell making me nauseous. After she blew it out, she looked at me. "You know I love you, Kar-Kar. Right?"

I nodded my little head. "Yes, Mommy. Please don't leave me in here, Mommy."

"You know why I have to, baby. If it doesn't hurt, you won't learn."

I felt confused. "What does that mean, Mommy?"

Her pale face smiled at me, a cruelness behind her eyes I had become used to. "I love you, Kar-Kar."

She closed the door, and I heard locks engage before I could ask anything more. I walked to the window and looked out to see the sun was quickly setting, and I hoped I wouldn't be left in here for days and days like I had been so many times.

And I didn't even know what I'd done to deserve it—just like all the times before.

"Shit, what's wrong with him?" I heard a voice say.

I blinked rapidly to see the three elves looking down at me. Embarrassed and confused, I stood quickly and shook off the . . . memory? "I'm . . . I'm okay."

Jalen measured me with a serious stare with his lavender eyes that were so much like mine. "You sure, dude?"

I nodded.

He looked at the other two, then back to me. "You know we're all related, right?"

I stopped in my tracks and looked at him. "You mentioned we were cousins in your email, but honestly, man, I don't remember much of my childhood. It sucks."

"There's a reason for that," Tarron replied, his arms folded over his massive chest covered in a blue and silver Havenwood Falls High hoodie.

I glanced at Jalen, then Tarron. "Why's that?"

Gavin, who had been mostly quiet this whole time, replied, "Magic, dude. You grew up here, but you left. Fuckin' witches put a spell around this place. You leave, your memories do, too. It sucks, but we all get why they do it."

"Witches . . ." I parroted. "There are witches here?"

The three of them burst into laughter. Finally, Jalen said, "Get some sleep. I'll be in the next room. There's a lot to discuss. And we'll do it tomorrow over pancakes and bacon."

The three of them left, and Jalen closed the door on his way out.

I glanced around the small room. One double bed, a dresser, a closet, and posters of my favorite female fitness model took up the entire wall of one side of the room.

I couldn't ever remember feeling this exhausted. I was so confused as to what was going on, where I was, and what I was feeling that I just couldn't process it. So after throwing my bag on the floor, taking off my jacket, and kicking off my shoes, I flipped the light off and fell onto the bed, passing out.

"He needs to come with us," I heard a voice whisper.

"No, fuck that. We need to get going," another voice said, trying to whisper, but failing miserably.

I blinked my eyes open and flipped back the covers. The room was strange to me, but I immediately recalled where I was. Still in yesterday's clothes, I slogged out of bed and went to see who was arguing outside the door. The voices had stopped, so I opened the door.

Two elves whipped their heads toward me.

"What's with all the noise?" I asked, stifling a yawn and scratching my head.

"Jalen's in jail, dude," Tarron replied, a look of stress coloring his young face.

I looked at Gavin, but pointed to Tarron. "Jail? You guys are shitting me, right?"

I couldn't explain the comfort and familiarity I felt in the presence of Gavin, but it was there.

"No, we're not shitting you. You remember us yet?" Gavin raked a hand through his hair.

Confused, but wanting to roll with it, I asked, "No. Should I?"

"Like I said," Gavin replied, "all in due time. But first things first. Meet us downstairs in ten."

He waved for Tarron to follow him down the stairs.

There was nothing worse than going to bed utterly confused, then waking up the same way. Sleeping was supposed to reset your brain. Make things clearer in the morning. But, apparently, that wasn't the case in Havenwood Falls.

After locking the door, I stripped off yesterday's clothes and wandered into the bathroom attached to my room for a shower.

CHAPTER 4

KARSON

"So what happened?" I asked as we rode in Gavin's Nissan sports car. I was sitting in the front seat, and Tarron was in the back.

Gavin lifted a shoulder and let it fall. "Dunno. After we all went to bed, I got a call from Jalen saying he'd been arrested and was in jail. I asked him why, but he just said he had to go. That was a few hours ago."

"Weird," I said, shaking my head.

"Get used to it." Tarron laughed.

"Ow!" A sudden burning pain in my neck caused me to slap my hand over it. I yanked the visor down and stared wide-eyed in the mirror at the tattoo of a phoenix that most certainly hadn't been there before. I was pretty tatted up, but chose to never get them on my neck.

Taron and Gavin started laughing.

"What in the hell is going on?" I asked, pointing to the tattoo and looking at them both incredulously.

"Your tat is back, man. That means your memories should shortly follow," Gavin responded.

"Finally," Tarron muttered from the backseat.

"What does this mean?" I asked, still confused, and the tattoo still burning like it was fresh.

Gavin held his arm out, and I stared at a tattoo of some kind of Celtic symbol. Tarron leaned forward and pulled up his sleeve to show me one he had on his forearm, a tree with roots extending down to his wrist. "Every resident gets a tat. Everyone. Even temporary ones. Ugh. Ya know what, just wait and pretty soon I won't have to explain shit."

"Fine," I said, huffing out a breath.

No wonder I left this weird-ass town. I looked again in the mirror and wanted to ask who had done the tattoo, as it was actually pretty awesome and quite badass, but I didn't.

We pulled up in front of the sheriff's station. It seemed pretty quiet, with two squad cars and a few unmarked vehicles in the front.

We wandered inside and spoke to a woman manning a desk. Gavin said, "Here to see Jalen Kane."

Without looking up, the woman kept her eyes on the computer screen and pointed at the door we'd just arrived in. "Just got taken to court."

"Crap," Gavin murmured.

"Is that bad?" I asked as we went back outside.

"I think I know what this is about," Tarron said. He glanced at me, then to Gavin. "Witches."

Gavin waved at us to follow. "That's what I was thinking, too."

I didn't ask. What would be the point? I'd find out soon enough. My head already felt like it might explode.

It was a short walk to the large, white building with the words *City Hall* boldly displayed on top. With bare trees and dead grass in front, I thought maybe in summer it looked much nicer with everything green. The sky was getting darker with bloated white clouds, and I could feel that it was going to start snowing soon. We walked to an unmarked door in the back of the building. There was an oddly familiar symbol of a half moon and a mountain above it. We went down a steep flight of stairs and through a room, which led to a large courtroom.

A panel of men and women sat at the front on a raised dais, and the one in the middle, an elegant-looking woman with silvery-white hair, seemed to be in charge. Jalen was sitting in front of them, his hands resting on a table.

The three of us took seats in the back of the courtroom as quietly as we could.

"This is just a preliminary hearing," said an older lady in a business suit, her graying hair in a bun. "The charge is breach of confidentiality among the supernatural; specifically, circumventing the systems put in place to protect the town by means of electronic hacking. How do you plead?"

I pulled my phone out and discreetly hit the email icon. I went to pull Jalen's email up, but it was gone. Not even in the trash. I looked in the sent items, and my reply had disappeared, too. Looking up, I realized the panel members were all supes, and suddenly realized what was going on. *He's here because of that email he sent me.*

I stood, but Gavin put his hand out to block me. "What are you doing?" he hissed.

"Move," I said, looking down at him menacingly.

His jaw ticked with annoyance, but he eventually moved his arm.

I slid out from the bench and approached the front. The panel members looked at me. A lady with dark brown hair smiled. "Welcome back, Karson."

How does she know my name?

Jalen turned and looked at me. "Go sit down. This isn't your problem."

I ignored him and looked at the panel. "Look, if he hadn't sent that email, there's no way I would have come back here. Can't you cut him a break?"

The panel members murmured amongst themselves, and the man spoke. He had a small bit of amusement dancing in his eyes. "Son, it's clear your memories have not returned, or else you would have known better than to approach the Court out of turn. So we will cut you some slack there. However, had we wanted to call character witnesses up, we would have. This is just a preliminary hearing, like I already said."

I had nothing to say to that, so I clapped my cousin on the shoulder and went to sit back down next to Gavin and Tarron.

"Mr. Kane, how do you plead?"

"Guilty, sir."

"Very well. Court will convene in three days for sentencing. The defendant shall remain remanded until the Court can ensure the internet wards are back in place and have been tested and reinforced. Court is dismissed." The man pounded his gavel.

Jalen looked at me apologetically as a young woman with glasses escorted him from the room.

The panel began to disperse, and I looked at Gavin and Tarron. "What now?"

Tarron looked at his watch. "I've already missed first period. I gotta go to school. I'll be over right after, as long as Willa doesn't have any plans."

He hurried out of the courtroom, and I looked at Gavin. "Willa?"

"His girlfriend. She's a wolf."

I made a face. "Really?"

He chuckled as we walked out of the room. "Yeah. Very weird, I know. But it works. Tarron's not full elven anyway."

"He's not?" I asked as we made our way down the hallway.

"No, he's . . . ya know what? You'll know soon enough," Gavin replied, shaking his head. "Let's go get something to eat."

"Now you're talking in a language I understand."

Gavin snorted.

CHAPTER 5

KARSON

*E*ggstravaganza was the coolest little breakfast shop I'd ever been in. Okay, well, maybe I had been here before, but I wouldn't know until, apparently, my stupid memories came back. Still, the place felt slightly familiar, just like every place else I'd been to so far in this town. The server set the check down. I grabbed it and insisted on paying, since Gavin had been chauffeuring me around town.

"Thanks, man," he said after I paid and we walked out. "Where do you want to go now?"

I wasn't sure. I measured him with a stare and said, "I hate to ask another question, but do you have a job or somewhere you need to be? It's Monday."

He chuckled. "Don't *you* have a job to be at?"

"The tattoo shop is closed on Sundays, Mondays, and Tuesdays. I'm good."

He nodded as we stopped outside a shop window displaying ski gear and clothing. "To answer your question, which you already know, I work doing online trading and stuff. With my boyfriend."

I lifted an eyebrow. "Well, that's awesome. Where's he now?"

"My boyfriend?" he asked, then started walking.

"Yes."

"In Denver. As you know. I only come here once a month so I don't forget this place. I grew up here, like you—with you. We're cousins. I'm Jalen's brother. But again"—he sighed—"you already know this."

I laughed. "Is there anything I can do to speed up the memory process thing?"

He shook his head. "Nah, it takes about twenty-four hours for elves. Last time I checked, anyway. In fact, you're lucky they didn't boot you out today for disrupting Court. Though there would be no use in that. No need to try to hide anything from you."

Again . . . weird. But okay. We kept walking, and I wasn't sure where we were going, but I was enjoying looking at the town, the familiarity mixed with newness kind of cool.

We passed by a building, a sign reading *Tragic Ink* in the second-story window. I pointed at it. "Tattoo shop?"

He nodded. "Don't go in there."

"Why not?" I asked.

He huffed. "I love you, man, but if you ask one more question, I'm gonna burn you."

"You can't use affliction on other elves," I stated matter-of-factly.

"Oh, I won't need that to inflict pain. Now, no more questions." He looked up at the sky. "It's cold as hell. You like video games?"

"Uh, yeah."

He grinned. "Let's go back to the house. Jalen's a video game tester. He's got every game you can think of."

I nodded. "Sounds cool. But aren't we . . . I mean, uh"—I needed to word this in the form of a non-question—"we should go bail him out first."

Gavin shook his head. "No bail in Havenwood Falls, man. He's gotta sit there till sentencing."

All righty then.

With Jalen in jail for at least three days, I wondered what I was supposed to do. I'd told my boss that I'd be back by Wednesday. Obviously, that wasn't going to happen.

Gavin and I had been playing *Call of Duty* and *PubG* for hours, eating junk food, when we decided to take a break. I looked outside and could see the sun was beginning to set.

"Can we go visit Jalen?" I asked, the bottle of Mountain Dew paused at my lips.

Gavin screwed off the lid to his water and looked at me. "Yeah, I guess. But why?"

This confused me, but I was careful not to ask another question. "I need to talk to him is all. About y'all's dad. He told me to come here because he needed help with him once he gets outta prison."

Gavin chuckled and took a swig. "He did not summon you here to help with our dad. That shitbag is beyond help."

My eyebrows hit my hairline. "Did you just call your dad a shitbag?"

He nodded. "Sure did."

"Okay. What about my parents? Where are they? I think I need to see them."

Gavin rolled his eyes. "Your dad is . . . Your mother . . . Fuck. When your memories are back, you can . . . I can't answer that."

We stared at each other for a few seconds, the tension in the air growing thick. "Okayyy. Well, tell me then, why do you not care that your brother's in jail?"

He set the bottle on the counter and put the lid back on. With a shake of his head, he looked at me. "You. Are. So. *Annoying*. Without. Your. Memories."

This pissed me off. The smug look on his face. The blasé attitude about his brother and my mental state. I was always a goal-minded person, so being here in this remote mountain town, seemingly without a reason, was driving me crazy.

"That doesn't make any sense!" I snapped. I wanted to fold the guy's teeth back with my fist. Instead, I turned around and punched the first thing I could see. Which, unfortunately for me, was an oven set into the wall of the kitchen. When my fist made contact, I watched as the black glass splintered and began to spiderweb.

As if in slow motion, I looked down at my fist and could see blood covering my knuckles and the bones of the top of my hand looking not quite right. Instead of being straight and symmetrical, the middle two were sort of askew. Then came the pain.

"Fuck!" I yelled, shaking out my bloodied hand.

Gavin raced over to me and looked down at my hand, then into my eyes. "Looks like a trip to the hospital is in your future, you dumbass hothead."

"I'm fine," I gritted, trying not to pant or pass out at the pain.

He scoffed. "Your hand is broken. You're not fine."

"It'll heal," I came back.

Gavin snatched a dishtowel and filled it with ice from the freezer, then handed it to me. He snatched his keys from the counter and demanded, "Get in the car."

I shook my head. "No. I'm fine. I'm sorry about the oven. I'll pay to have it fixed. This ice pack will be just fine. I'll be okay."

"If you don't get your stubborn ass in the car by the time I count to ten, I'm gonna call Tarron over here, and we're going to drag your ass to the hospital. And trust me, you don't want that."

The pain in my hand was getting worse, and I was trying to smile in spite of it. "I'm not afraid of a high school kid."

"Don't let the baby face fool you," Gavin said, shoving me toward the front door.

Deciding I wasn't going to win this fight, and hoping the hospital bill wasn't going to break my bank account, I let Gavin corral me to the car.

I wasn't sure why I was fixated on her braids, but I was. Their auburn color was almost mesmerizing. Or maybe I was using them as a focal point in order to not cry out in pain. *Scottlin*, the name sewed onto her white doctor's coat read.

Yeah, my hand was broken. The middle two bones were fractured, and it was for this reason I sat here waiting for someone to come and get me so they could put my hand in a cast.

"Are you in any pain?" the pretty redhead asked me.

I shook my head slowly. Of course I had to put on a brave face and lie through my teeth. "It's not too bad."

She lifted her gaze to mine, and I almost choked on my own breath. Her eyes were so blue, I thought maybe the sky outside the window was reflecting off them.

"So how did you do this, Mr. Kane?" Scottlin asked sweetly, her voice like a soft melody floating on a breeze.

It seemed I had two choices here: The truth, or something way cooler. After staring into her face, I decided on something in between. "I punched something."

She laughed and shook her head. "Well, that's pretty evident."

"Is it?" I asked, just anxious to keep her talking. She had a sweet disposition about her, but she also had that hot nurse thing going on.

"It is. It's not easy to break the metacarpals when the hand isn't balled into a fist. Unless something falls down on it and crushes it, of course."

When she lifted those baby blues to mine, I could hardly remember a word she'd said. "Huh?"

Laughing again, she said, "Keep your arm still and stay here. I'll be right back."

I wanted to laugh. Really, where was I gonna go?

She came back a couple minutes later with something that looked like a board and a roll of tape. I looked at the device, then back into her face. I could see a light smattering of freckles there.

After grinning at me, she slid the board under my arm. "You wanna do this the hard way or the easy way?"

I looked at her. "The easy way. You've got an easy button, right?"

She grinned and, seeming to produce a syringe out of nowhere, she lifted the sleeve on my right arm and tore open an alcohol swab. I watched as her brow furrowed.

"What?" I asked. "I'm not afraid of needles."

She pointed to my tattoos. "That's obvious."

Then she swabbed a small section above the skull on my shoulder. After pushing the plunger home, she removed the needle and quickly put a Band-Aid on it.

"Let's give the meds a few minutes to kick in."

I couldn't stop staring at her. "Are you going to stay and keep me company?"

I immediately felt relaxed and happy, like I'd taken a hit off a joint.

She bit back a grin. "You're funny."

"And you're pretty," I replied quickly.

"Thank you," she said quietly. "I'll be right back."

I watched her leave and wished she wasn't wearing the medical smock so I could check out her ass.

"She's got a boyfriend," Gavin said from the corner of the room, where I had forgotten he was seated. He was looking down at his phone, typing something.

"Really. Is he hotter than me?" I asked, now feeling totally high and not caring about filtering my mouth.

Gavin chuckled. "I'm only saying this because I like dudes and not because you're my cousin, but fuck no. He's a total dweeb."

"Human?" I asked.

Gavin looked toward the door and then back to me. "Keep your voice down!"

I furrowed my brow. "I was."

He laughed again and shook his head. "No, you weren't. And yes, the dude is human."

"No, is the hot nurse human?"

He glanced toward the door again, then back to me with his lavender-colored eyes. "Not sure. Also, she's not a nurse. She's a nurse practitioner."

Cocking my head to the side, I asked, "What's the difference? Hot nurse is a hot nurse."

"Oh, my gods. You without your memories is bad enough, but you loaded on pain meds is like, torture."

"I'm not loaded," I practically slurred.

"A nurse practitioner is almost like a doctor. I think. Something like that."

Just then, the cutie with the braids came back in. "How are you feeling, Mr. Kane?"

"Hey," I asked, "are you a doctor?"

She grinned and looked at my hand. "No, but kind of close."

"Do you know me?" I asked.

"Oh, brother," Gavin groaned from the corner.

She looked into my eyes. "No, should I?"

I blew out an exaggerated breath. "I don't know. My memories are . . ." I made circles near my temple with my finger and whistled.

She looked alarmed and shot a look to Gavin. "He's from here?"

I looked at Gavin, and now there were two of him as he said, "Yes, just got back into town early this morning."

She flicked her gaze to me and then pulled out a flashlight. As she shined it into my eyes, her light ginger brows furrowed together. She clicked the light off and returned it to her pocket. Then she glanced at Gavin again. "Pain meds mixed with the spell is never a good idea. I wish I had been informed."

"Oh, no," I slurred, putting my hand on her arm. "I'm okay. I really am." I reached up and fingered a braid. "You're sooo pretty."

She shook her head and looked at Gavin, concerned.

"I need to lie down." I let my top half fall back on the gurney I had been sitting on. The last thing I heard was the nurse's beautiful voice saying, "After I'm done, get him home. Then call me."

CHAPTER 6

SCOTTLIN

*a*s I slogged into the house, exhausted as usual, my phone vibrated. I wearily pulled it from the pocket of my scrubs and could see I had a text.

Len: Can I come over?

Me: Sorry, not tonight.

I closed and locked the door behind me, then set my purse, keys, and jacket on the dining room table. Glancing at the microwave clock, I could see it was past eleven p.m.

Why do I work so many hours?

Shaking my head, I headed toward my room and stripped off my scrubs. I put them in the special hamper I used for my medical clothes. Then I wandered into the bathroom and turned on the water before lighting the two vanilla-scented candles on the vanity. I guessed I was an odd one—I preferred to shower in the dark and quiet. It helped me unwind, I supposed.

Once the water was heated, I stepped into the shower and groaned as the heat pounded my stressed muscles. With the flats of my hands against the wall and the water cascading over me, I closed my eyes and willed the relaxation of the shower to melt all the troubles of the day away.

I hadn't been working at the Havenwood Falls Medical Center very long, which was why I was on ER duty. And I was okay with that. It had been barely a year since I'd gotten my degree to become an NP, and I knew I had to pay my dues. However, the ER could be a sad and stressful place.

But it wasn't the sad or stressful that now invaded my brain. It was the smoking hot elven guy with the broken hand I'd worked on. The way his lavender-colored eyes had pierced me while we had been talking. The strain of his black Guns N' Roses T-shirt over thick, muscular, tattooed arms. It was all I could do to keep eye contact with the guy.

I turned around, grabbed my strawberry-scented shampoo, and squirted some into my hands. While working it into my hair, I thought more about Karson Kane. He had apparently just returned back to town after a long time away, and didn't have his memories back. Then, like an idiot, I went and injected him with ten milligrams of morphine to relieve his pain. Huge no-no. Narcotics combined with powerful witch spells had to be considered very carefully when used.

I should have asked him more questions.

I should have been more thorough.

I should have asked his elven friend about Karson's situation beforehand.

Dammit! I should have known better.

I was glad that, at least, I had found out about his memories before I had decided to heal him magically. Still, I wish I would have known he had just returned to town and was still an amnesiac.

Deciding that self-loathing was too much of an energy-suck, I rinsed off and stepped out of the shower. Once toweled dry, I padded into my room and slipped on a black tank top with *Book Nerd* written in blue across the chest and a pair of comfy black yoga pants.

After combing out my wet hair, I sat on the bed and looked at my phone, staring at the text from Len asking me if everything was all right. I felt bad for ignoring him. Truth was, I had been delaying the inevitable with him for quite some time. We'd been dating about six months, but I just wasn't feeling it. It was one of those things where you knew the other person was way more into you than you were into them. And I felt bad about that. Really bad. But I couldn't force what wasn't there. Len, a volunteer firefighter and EMT who worked for the town, had asked me out one day after he'd brought a patient into the ER. He had been cute and charming, and I'd agreed to meet him for coffee.

Since then, we had been seeing each other, but we had never become serious—and there was a reason for that. There was no chemistry. I didn't give myself to just anyone, and when sparks were lacking, there was no way I was going to.

It was for this reason that I had been dreading doing what I had to do—break up with him. But I wasn't going to do it over text, and I was certainly too exhausted to meet with him in person. *Tomorrow*, I told myself. *I'll deliver the bad news on my lunch break.*

Frowning, and with my stomach in knots, my thumbs typed out a reply:

I'm fine. Let's meet for lunch at Napoli's at noon tomorrow.

His reply was immediate: **I'll be there, beautiful.**

I groaned. This was going to completely suck.

My knee bounced up and down as I sat in a corner table at Napoli's Pizza. I wasn't hungry, and knew I wouldn't be able to eat, but I had to order something while I waited for Len to show up. I was fifteen minutes early, and, as he was always late, I knew I would be sitting here for a while. *Good.* It would give me time to formulate what I wanted to say, because as of now, I had nothing but pure lameness planned.

"What can I get ya?" I heard an accented voice ask.

I looked up to see a young, olive-skinned girl standing there in a Napoli's T-shirt and jeans. My eyes flicked to her nametag.

I smiled. "Hi, Zara, can I get a coffee and a water please?"

"Absolutely, miss," she replied, smiling at me.

Her British accent was a little odd-sounding in Havenwood Falls, but then again, nothing about this place was normal. Staring unseeing at the menu, I went over a million different ways to word what I had to say to my boyfriend in my head. Nothing sounded good, and I grew frustrated. Unfortunately, for once, I was out of time, it seemed. I heard the bell above the door chime and looked up to see Len walking in. He smiled immediately when he saw me.

He does have such a nice smile . . . Maybe I should give it more time.

Stop, Scottlin. Just stop!

I stood when he arrived at my table. He hugged me, then kissed me on the cheek like he always did. After he sat down, Zara returned with my drinks and asked Len what he wanted.

Diet Coke with a lime.

"Diet Coke with a lime," he replied, smiling.

Zara grinned. "You got it, love."

"I wasn't aware we had any people from England living here. Well, besides Dr. Lewis's family," I said quietly as she walked away.

Len chuckled. "She's American. She's from Havenwood Falls. She just loves to speak with a British accent. Maybe she wants to be an actress?"

My eyes widened. "Seriously? Well, someone give that girl an Oscar. She had me convinced."

Len chuckled. "Right?"

I cleared my throat and looked down at the menu again. "You going to get pizza, or something else?"

When he didn't answer, I looked up at him over my menu. He was staring at me, his chocolate-brown eyes almost studying me.

"What?" I asked.

"What, what?" he countered. "You asked me here. You never ask me to lunch. Plus, you know it's my day off, or else I wouldn't have been able to meet you at all."

I sighed, set the menu down, then folded my hands over it. "We need to talk."

"You're breaking up with me," he deadpanned.

Chewing the side of my lip, I began to nod slowly when Zara returned with his soda.

"You ready to order?" she asked, still in character.

I shook my head. "No, not yet."

Sensing the tension, she simply nodded and flounced off.

Len made a scoffing noise and looked down at his own hands. "I'm not stupid, you know. I know this has been a long time coming."

"I'm sorry," I squeaked. "But it has."

His gaze met mine once again. "No, I'm sorry. I fell much harder than I should have. For you."

"Len, it's not your f—"

He put a hand up. "I know it's not. But you can't force what's not there."

"You took the words right out of my mouth," I whispered.

He looked pained, but somehow relieved, too, as he said, "You're a beautiful girl, Scottlin. You'll find someone. I'm just sorry it isn't me."

This hurt my heart even more, and I felt like a total jerk. "I'm sorry."

"Can we stay friends?" he asked. "Still have lunch?"

This made me happy. I thought guys hated it when you friend-zoned them. "Yes. I would love that."

Zara returned to take our order. I wasn't sure I could eat, but I decided on a house salad and a slice of cheese pizza. Len got a calzone, and once she walked away, he started a conversation about the upcoming election in Havenwood Falls, and how strange it was that a Stuart always won the mayor's seat. I don't think we'd ever had such an easygoing interaction before.

I felt relief I didn't deserve.

CHAPTER 7

KARSON

I woke the next morning feeling like I'd drunk a fifth of Jack. Groaning, I rolled over and looked for the alarm clock that wasn't there. Opening my eyes further, I realized I wasn't at home, but in a strange bed. Light from a window illuminated the room, and once I located my phone, I plucked it from the nightstand. It was after ten a.m., and I wondered how I'd gotten here and why I'd slept so long.

Jalen's house. The hospital. The cute redhead.

I pulled my hand out from under the comforter and examined the cast covering it. "Shit," I groaned.

So it had been real. I'd punched the oven in the kitchen and broken my hand. What in the hell was going on? Just then, I put my good hand to my neck, remembering the phoenix tattoo. I got out of bed and rushed to the bathroom to stare in the mirror. Sure, I'd inked that bird with its flame many times on many people, but I'd never thought of getting a phoenix tat myself. I opened the door to my room and wandered down the stairs. There was nobody around. Shrugging, I opened the refrigerator and found a box of pizza with a few slices in it.

I could eat cold pizza, but I couldn't do a no-coffee morning. While I munched on a slice, I rummaged through the cabinets and located some coffee pods, plunking one in the single-cup maker. Looking around at my surroundings, I could tell the house was older, but it had been furnished and decorated nicely. Ironically, it was how I would decorate a house if I had one. As of now, I only had a one-bedroom apartment in Colorado Springs that wasn't worth spending too much money on.

Speaking of . . .

I'd been here well over twenty-four hours, and I was still confused as hell. Maybe Jalen had been lying in his email. Maybe he'd said all that stuff to get me into town, playing on my loneliness.

But . . . how would he have known about me or my life?

I was getting a headache from this shit.

The blue lights lit up the coffee machine, and I slammed the lid down, placed a coffee mug with the words *I Love Havenwood Falls* printed on it, and pushed the button to start the blasted machine. I definitely did not love Havenwood Falls at the moment. I just wanted to go home.

But you are home came a voice. Inside my head.

Irritated with all my fleeting thoughts, I watched as the machine spit out the black liquid, and as soon as the cup was full, I picked it up and carried the mug upstairs and had drunk most of it by the time I reached the bathroom. I took a shower, cautious not to get my cast wet.

After drying off, I stared at myself in the mirror, my purple eyes gazing back at me.

"Who are you?" I whispered.

Of course, I knew who I was. My name was Karson Eli Kane, I was twenty-four years old, and I worked as a tattoo artist. I lived in Colorado Springs. I liked women, and they liked me. I was damn good at what I did, and I had a few friends and a super cool boss.

Looking down at my cast, I shook my head. But where did I go to high school? Where had I grown up? Who were my parents? Had I had a happy childhood with a dog or a cat? What about siblings—did I have any? The fleeting memory of that weird blackout I'd had came back to me, but when I tried to remember exactly what it had been about, the images vanished, like a vapor.

I looked down at the tattoos covering my arms and could still see the small, circular scars under them. You had to look closely to see them, but they were there. I just couldn't remember how I got them or what they were from.

Sighing, I left the bathroom and threw on a Metallica T-shirt with a thick hoodie over it. After sliding on my jeans and shoving my feet into boots, I quickly scrubbed my teeth and threw some goop into my hair to make it stand up the way I liked. Some hair stuff had gotten onto the silver hoop in my right ear, and I wiped it off.

I headed downstairs and out the door, not having ever seen another member of the household. Of course, I knew Jalen was in jail, and that was where I was headed—to get some damn answers. I just hoped it was visiting hours by the time I got there.

On foot, I walked out of the neighborhood and soon found myself on the main street of the town. The strange feeling of not knowing where I was, yet knowing exactly where I was, was completely odd. I felt like I had some kind of war battling inside my head.

The storefronts, shops, cars, and streets were comforting and familiar, yet I couldn't remember where I was supposed to go to reach the jail. Was it inside City Hall?

Oh yeah, it's at the sheriff's station. Where was that again?

As I passed a small pizza shop, I casually glanced inside. I could see a few people having lunch. That's when she caught my eye: the gorgeous nurse practitioner from the night before. She ran her fingers along her hair that lay over her shoulder as she laughed at whatever the guy she was with had said. I paused to watch them as he reached over and grabbed her hand. She looked down at the interaction and seemed to frown briefly.

Damn. Guess Gavin was right about the boyfriend. It would have been nice to take her out and get to know her. Guess that's not going to happen.

Before I turned to walk away, our eyes met. Hers widened momentarily when she spotted me, then she smiled. I didn't think she'd recognize me. She motioned for me to come into the restaurant, but . . . fuck that. I already had some dumb little schoolboy crush on her. I had no desire to meet her boyfriend, or husband, or whoever the hell that was.

Looking away, I quickly made my way toward the jail. I reached City Hall first and stopped short as I looked at the massive structure.

"Karson," a high-pitched voice said from behind me.

I turned around to see Scottlin standing there with her hands in her pockets and a friendly smile on her pale face. Her bright indigo eyes looked extra striking against the cloudy gray sky.

"Uh"—her gaze flicked down—"how's your hand?"

My eyes lazily drifted down to it, then back to her gorgeous face. I looked at her strawberry braids and wondered how fun it would be pull them while . . .

"I can see you're busy," she cut into my thoughts.

Jerking back to reality, my eyes widened. "No."

Her ginger brows furrowed. "No . . . what?"

"Shit." I shook my head. "No, not busy. And fine. My hand's fine."

No, it wasn't. It was throbbing something fierce in this cold-ass weather. But no way was I gonna puss out and tell her that.

"Really?" she asked, taking another step toward me. I noticed she wore green medical scrubs under her oversized brown jacket, which had white fur trim around the collar and sleeves.

"Yes, really."

"Can I take a look?" she asked, with a lopsided smile on her cherry-red lips.

I shook my head. "Nah, I'm good. But . . . could you tell me where the jail is at?"

We were within touching distance now. And, oh, how I wanted to touch her, but knew there was no use in doing that.

"It's on the other side of City Hall."

"Thanks," I replied, turning to continue walking.

"Why are you going to the jail?" she asked.

I stopped and turned around, thrusting my hands into the pocket of my hoodie, the cast barely fitting inside. "Why do you care? Isn't your man waiting for you back there?"

God, Karson, could you sound any more insecure? I turned around and walked away.

"If you're referring to the guy in Napoli's, he's . . . just a friend."

"Famous last words," I murmured. I figured while I was making an ass of myself, I might as well win an Oscar at it.

She laughed at my stupidity. "He's an ex. Not that it's any of your business."

Turning around, I could see her walking back toward the restaurant. I longed to run after her and rub my thumbs over her cheeks—ones that looked to be turning red from the cold. But, of course, I didn't. I let her go and headed toward the jail.

CHAPTER 8

SCOTTLIN

*Y*eah, I was a really bad person. A total ass.

The second I'd seen Karson Kane's gaze piercing mine from the other side of the window, I'd excused myself, jumped up from my seat in Napoli's, and bolted for the door. I couldn't believe I'd even remembered to grab my coat from the back of the chair.

Len must have picked up the tab and left, because by the time I arrived back there, he was gone, and the table we'd occupied was clean and ready for more patrons.

Yep, I'm an ass.

With a shake of my head, I walked back toward the Havenwood Falls Medical Center, knowing I'd taken a lot more than an hour lunch break. But if my boss tried to give me any crap about it, I'd remind him that I never took lunch breaks. Sure, I'd go down to Coffee Haven and grab something every once in a while, but I always ate it in my small office where I was probably typing my patient notes into the computer. I hadn't actually left the facility for a lunch break in . . . well, ever. Not in the almost year I'd worked there. I hadn't even finished my lunch before taking off after Karson, but thankfully, the four bites of pizza and half a salad I'd managed were enough. And now, as I sat in my office, I needed to finish my notes before I had to head back into the ER.

I typed what I had jotted down about Karson's case.

Subject is a twenty-four-year-old elven male. He presents to the ER with hand pain. Suspects fracture. Subject reports he struck a glass oven door with a closed fist no less than one hour prior to arriving at the ER.

I lifted my gaze from the page and stared at the door to my office. Why had he punched something? Was this guy a hothead?

I finished my notes and decided, while I was taking one-hour-and-fifteen-minute lunches, that I could break another rule today and maybe look him up in the hospital's computer.

After a few keystrokes into the part of the computer only we supernatural staff had access to, his name popped up right away. Karson Eli Kane: Elven. Date of birth, hair and eye color, parents' names and race (both purebred elven). He didn't have much else in there. Born and raised in Havenwood Falls. No significant medical history or problems. Everyone in town knew about the Kanes, but I had never personally met Karson. I was thinking maybe it was time I asked around about this guy.

I sat back in my chair, my pencil to my mouth, and pondered this. *Why do I give a crap? He's just some hot guy I treated.* Sure, he had acted a little macho, like the broken hand hadn't hurt, but I had seen that plenty of times, especially in male supes. Men—they just couldn't seem to embrace pain.

They weren't like us women. We not only embraced pain, we bathed in it and made it our friend. We wallowed in and clung to the agony like it was our long-lost friend. And for what? Why did we do this? I wasn't sure, but I definitely did not want to think about pain right now. My breakup with Len—which had gone way too easily, I might add—was still fresh in my mind. The pathetic part was that I should be feeling pain. I should be feeling guilty. I should be feeling a loss.

Except for a little guilt, I felt none of these things.

The only thing I felt was a draw to the tall, sexy blond elf who'd come into my ER yesterday. I thought about our interaction in the town square earlier and couldn't believe he was the same guy. One had been broken and in need of help. The other had been cocky, moody, broody, and a little emotional, if I was being honest.

Move on, Scottlin. You're twenty-four. There are lots of fish in the sea.

Pushing thoughts of him from my mind, I clicked on the next patient file and began typing. I definitely needed the distraction.

I ended up staying way too late at the hospital. It seemed like the work just never ended, and I had always been the type who liked to finish what I started before leaving for the day. But after almost a year here, it was clear that was never going to happen.

You wouldn't think a small town like Havenwood Falls would have such a high amount of ER visits, but we did. The problem was, while the human ailments were easy to fix, it was the supes who came in with odd injuries or symptoms that sometimes left us scratching our heads. Like this one, as I began to type, since dictation was forbidden here, in case humans overheard us:

Subject is a seventeen-year-old female, suspected wolf, but no lycan characteristics have presented as of yet. Patient claims to have fevers daily, but no other symptoms. Ran routine tests, including CBC . . .

With a yawn, I saved the file, put it into the queue, and began to shut down the computer when a notification popped up that Karson's lab results were ready from when the nurse had taken his blood upon his admission to the ER.

Just read it later, I told myself.

Of course, I couldn't help myself and clicked on it. I casually read over the results and was about to close the file when something caught my eye.

I squinted at the screen. My eyes widened. How in the heck did he have molomorphine in his system? That was only for vampires!

There was only one answer: Someone had prepared ten milligrams of molomorphine into the syringe—not the regular morphine I'd ordered. I'd need to check the nurse's schedule to see who'd prepared it.

In the meantime, how was an elf even functioning on molomorphine? I scanned Karson's medical record and could not find a phone number. All patients admitted into the emergency room were supposed to leave one. Yet more incompetence of the ER admin staff I was going to have to bring up with the hospital administrator.

Let it go, Scottlin. Let it go.

I took a deep breath and tried to rein in my inability to let go of control. "Just think of another way around this," I murmured.

Remembering reading in his file that he was a cousin to the Kanes, I knew I could easily find a phone number for one of them. Those boys were constantly getting hurt. I specifically remembered last winter when Jalen Kane thought he could jump off a gondola while it was still several feet in the air and just ski down the hill. Unfortunately for him, it hadn't worked out that well, and a broken ankle was his reward. Lucky for him, the elven healed quickly—not as quickly as vampires or wolves, but with some help from me, he avoided wearing a cast altogether.

I grinned at the memory and went into the hospital's database to find Jalen's phone number. I found it quickly and dialed his cell first, but it went straight to voicemail, as if it were dead. Next, I tried what was listed as a home number. After two rings, somebody picked up.

"Hello?" answered a deep male voice.

I cleared my throat. "Hello, may I speak to Karson Kane?"

After a long pause, the voice said, "He's not here. May I take a message?"

"Sure, but who am I speaking with?" I asked.

"Gavin. I'm Karson's cousin. And you are?"

"I'm Scottlin Glover. I'm a nurse practitioner here at the Havenwood Falls Medical Center. Karson was recently treated in our ER, and I'm calling to follow up with him."

Gavin chuckled. "Yeah, I know. Dumbass punched the oven. It's all cracked now."

I furrowed my brow. "Okay, well, do you possibly have a phone number I could use to reach him?"

"Sure. Hang on." I could hear the phone rustling, then he came back and recited a number very quickly.

"Seven-one-nine area code?" I asked.

"Yes," he replied. "That's his cell."

"Thank you, Gavin."

"No problem."

I hung up and dialed his number. The 719 area code was southern Colorado. Where had this guy come from?

CHAPTER 9

KARSON

*J*alen stood inside his cell, metal bars separating us. He looked happy to see me. I gave him a quick fist-bump, then slipped him two flowers I'd swiped from a vase at the hospital yesterday.

"Thanks," he said, popping them into his mouth and chewing quickly.

I folded my arms across my chest as I measured my "cousin" with a hard glare. "Now. You wanna tell me just what the hell is going on here?"

Jalen had the decency to look embarrassed. "I'm sorry, man. I didn't anticipate this." He gestured around the jail with his eyes. "Dad's getting released soon, and I just needed a little help."

I blew out a breath and raked my fingers through my too-long hair. "Help with what? Do I look like a damn social worker? What can I do?"

"No," he said, looking as if he was about to snap. "I just . . . I needed you here." He looked down. "What happened to your hand?"

All this cryptic talk and odd, unfinished conversation was working my last nerve. I ignored his question. "Look, dude. I don't know you at all. You send me this weird-ass email to get me to come to this weird-ass town, and once I get here—"

Jalen cut me off. "What are you talking about? Are you seriously standing there and telling me you still don't remember this place? What's wrong with you, Karson? You were born and raised here! Your memories should have returned by now. Something isn't right."

I stared at him incredulously and then took a few steps back, preparing to leave. "I still have no idea what you mean, so I think I'm just gonna go catch a bus back to the Springs and get on with my life. I have a shitload of clients waiting for tats, and I don't have time for these bitch-ass games."

"Wait!" Jalen said, sounding desperate.

I stopped and turned around. "What?"

"You don't remember anything? Nothing at all?"

I needed to come clean and tell him that yes, some of the things in the town felt familiar to me, almost comforting. But I couldn't explain it, and I doubted he could, either. So I changed the subject. "When are you getting out of here?"

"Don't know. I'll be here at least two more days, though," he replied.

I sighed. "What am I supposed to do in the meantime?"

He blew out a breath and jutted his chin at the phoenix. "Tattoo returned, I see."

"Yep. Weird as hell, since I don't remember getting it."

"You will. Just strange that you haven't remembered us yet. Something is wrong. You should probably go find—"

"Visiting time is over," a deep voice bellowed.

I glanced at the deputy, who sat at a nearby desk with a Styrofoam cup in his hand. I looked back at Jalen. "That's my cue to leave."

"Find a witch. They can figure out why your memories haven't returned," Jalen called out.

"Shut the hell up!" the deputy snapped, getting up from his desk and rushing over to Jalen.

I watched wide-eyed as he unlocked the cell door, tossed him onto the stone bench, and told him there'd be consequences if he didn't keep his mouth shut.

The deputy then locked the door, mumbled something about the Kanes, looked at me and snarled, "Get out of here!"

I backed out of the sheriff's station and sprinted down the road that would lead me to my cousins' house.

If that was who they truly were.

As I slowed to a stroll on the snowy, icy streets, plumes of breath clouding as I walked, I pulled my cell from my pocket. Before I could swipe the screen to check it, it suddenly rang in my hand with an unknown number.

"Hello?"

"Karson Kane?"

"Yeah, who's this?"

"Hi, Karson, it's Scottlin." She cleared her throat. "From Havenwood Falls Medical Center. I treated you earlier . . ."

Like she needed to explain who she was. How could I forget that hottie? "What can I do for you?"

"Well, I've come across something in your medical file that needs to be re-checked. Can you come back to the medical center?"

Figuring I had nothing else to do, I shrugged a shoulder. "Sure. When?"

A long pause, and she replied, "Uh, now, if you can."

"Fine. I'll be there in a few." I ended the call and turned around. I knew I needed to head west to reach it. How I knew that, I wasn't sure. I just did.

My head was swirling with all kinds of things. My conversation with Jalen, which had gotten me nowhere. All the work I was missing out on back home and how I would pay my rent next month. Jalen's alarm at how I hadn't "gotten my memories back."

That disturbed me. I was an elf. I knew that things weren't as they seemed. After all, my ears were pointed, but nobody could see that. They were glamoured from humans. Magic. I knew there were witches and vampires and wolves—God, so many wolves in Colorado. But we supes kept to ourselves and never mingled or bothered with the other species except when we had to. Hell, I even had a special ink for the vampires who came in for tats. I had to use a very small needle and work very quickly to tattoo them, or else the ink would spread, then disappear on their skin. But I had found a way to get it to stick because I was awesomely talented that way. Also, there may have been a little magic involved.

The vampires and other creatures who came into the shop to see me knew what I was. They always did, but it was obviously never discussed. Occasionally, I would get small talk from one, asking me where I was from. But I could never tell them because I couldn't remember. It was like the back of my mind had all this information stored, but the front of it was clouded with a thick blanket of fog and wouldn't allow the information to come forward.

I had been musing as I walked, and now found myself in front of the Havenwood Falls Medical Center. I entered in through the front door and made my way to the emergency room.

A cheery young girl—witch—in scrubs greeted me with a smile on her face. She slid some jet-black hair behind her ear that had fallen out of her hair clip. "Hi. Can I help you?"

"Yeah. Looking for Dr. . . . I'm looking for Nurse . . ." I furrowed my brow. "Got an employee named Scottlin here?"

Her pretty face lit up. "Yeah, she's our nurse practitioner on call. I'll let her know you're here. Name?"

Oh yeah. "Karson," I grunted.

I watched as she picked up the phone and punched some numbers. "Yes, ma'am. A, uh, Karson is here to see you." Pause. "Will do."

She hung up and looked at me once more. "Go down the hall, last door on the right." She gestured toward the wide wooden door that seemed to lead into the offices area of the hospital.

I thanked her and pushed open the door, hoping Scottlin could give me some answers. It was, after all, the only reason I agreed to come back here. I couldn't be here in this town not understanding why everyone expected me to remember them, but feeling so at ease and comfortable here at the same time.

Nope. Nope. Nope. I was gonna get some answers. Today.

I found a door with a plaque displaying her name and knocked twice.

"Come in," I heard her call out.

I twisted the doorknob and pushed the door open. She sat behind a desk wearing a white medical coat, her hands folded together over the top of the desk.

"Have a seat." She glanced at the chairs in front of her desk.

I obeyed, sitting in one of the plush, red chairs.

Piercing me with a stare, she asked, "How are you feeling?"

Caught off guard by her question, I simply lifted a shoulder and put on an impassive mask. "Fine. Why?"

"Your memories return?" she asked.

I stared at her long and hard for a moment before replying, "No."

"Nothing at all? Don't you think that's a bit strange?" she countered.

I snorted. "Lady, this whole town is strange. Jalen told me in an email that I was born and raised here. That my memories of the town would return. Well, they haven't. So I'm beginning to think this whole weird-ass place is just a figment of my fuckin' imagination."

She laughed softly and looked down at something on her desk. "It's not, Mr. Kane. I can assure you."

I huffed. "Scottlin, look at me."

She lifted her sapphire gaze questioningly to meet mine.

"Don't call me Mr. Kane. Just Karson. Okay?"

"Okay," she replied, staring into my eyes.

CHAPTER 10

SCOTTLIN

I bit back a smile. *Wow, bossy, this one.*

"Do you know me?" he asked, still piercing me with those gorgeous purple-blue eyes. They reminded me of the sky at night during a storm, where you could only see its color when the lightning illuminated it briefly. Probably because the storm behind his gaze was just as violent and beautiful.

I shook my head, remembering he'd asked me that before. Right after I had administered the narcotic. "I don't, but I know your cousins."

"Are you from here?" he asked, and I noticed he was absentmindedly rubbing his hand over the cast.

I glanced back into his eyes. "My family moved here when I was ten. I was raised out by the falls, and was homeschooled by my mom and grandmother. I didn't meet a lot of people, really, until I went to college."

He nodded. "So what did you need to see me for?"

I looked down at his hand, then back to his face. I had to keep my eyes trained on his in order not to stare at his full lips. "Your hand is bothering you, I can see. Being elven, you should heal quicker than most."

Karson raised an eyebrow at me. "How did you know that? I thought you were human."

Only partially. I pointed to the computer screen. "It's in your medical record."

He lowered his voice. "So the humans around here know about us?"

There was no way to answer that without getting complicated, so I said, "No, not really. Only supes can see those notations in your record. To a normal human, that part would read your race, such as White, or Hispanic, or whatever."

"To answer your question, yes, it still hurts, but the cold isn't helping."

I got up, walked to the cabinet, and pulled open a hand warmer pouch. I shook it to activate it, then wrapped it in a small hand towel. I placed it on his hand and told him to hold it there. I wished I could just heal him now, but I wasn't taking that chance. Not with his amnesia still in effect.

He looked up at me from where he sat, and his features softened. "Thank you. That feels better already."

"You're welcome." I smiled warmly at him. "I'll give you a few more before you leave. You shouldn't be walking around in this cold anyway. You don't have a car?"

"I do, but it has a busted transmission. I'm saving up to fix it. So I walk or Uber everywhere back in the Springs. Took a Greyhound to get here."

"I see," I replied. "Well, I wanted to let you know that I believe you received a pretty large dose of a narcotic yesterday when you came in. The nurse grabbed the one infused with magic for vampires, called molomorphine. Vampires heal pretty quickly, but there are times they need something immediately for the pain, so that was our, ah, special blend, if you will. It should *not* have been used on you, and I wanted to apologize for the mix-up. You seem to be feeling okay, though?"

"That might explain the brain fog. I thought it was just this memory problem that was doing it. And being in a strange place that doesn't feel so strange sometimes."

I licked my lips and measured my words carefully. "Actually, I have reason to believe the narcotic might be affecting the memory spell. The wards the witches put around the town are quite complex, and very specific. Sure, they affect each person differently, but eventually, everyone remembers. And maybe you will, too, and just need more time, but I can't help but think the molomorphine you received is delaying their return. Magic messing with other magic. I could send you to see Addie, or we can wait and see what happens."

He nodded and almost looked relieved. Then I noticed a new tattoo on his neck that wasn't there yesterday. "Resident tattoo?"

He put his hand to his neck and nodded. "Just appeared outta nowhere."

I rolled up the sleeve on my right arm to show him the shadowed blue butterfly on my inner wrist. "Here's mine."

Karson sat forward in his chair and looked at it. "May I?"

I nodded.

He gently took my wrist and brought it close to his face. Then he rubbed his thumb over it. The motion caused my entire body to break out in goosebumps, and I resisted the shudder that wanted to overtake me.

"Beautiful." He looked up at me.

"Thank you. Addie does good work."

He let go of my wrist and sat back in the chair. "You've mentioned her twice now. She's a tattoo artist and a witch, or what?"

I laughed. "I guess you could say that. She's kind of in charge of the town wards and keeping our little place here a true haven. She works with the Court."

He nodded, but said nothing. I could tell he was trying to figure everything out.

"Would you mind if I did a quick exam?" I asked.

He lifted a shoulder and let it fall. "No, go ahead."

I stood up and went around the desk, coming to stand in front of him.

"Do you need me to stand up, or what?"

"No, you can stay seated." I pulled my flashlight from the pocket of my lab coat, bent slightly, and shone it in his eyes quickly. Normal pupil dilation. I replaced the flashlight, then removed the stethoscope from around my neck. "Please sit up as straight as you can."

Karson did as I asked, and I listened to his lungs and his heart. The heartbeat was a tad slow, but he was a big guy—about six foot two and over two hundred pounds—and he still obviously had the narcotic in his system. I removed the stethoscope and put it back around my neck. Then I knelt down in front of him and felt his throat. No swelling. Without getting up, I looked at him and asked, "Are you in any pain?"

He shook his head slowly. "Just the hand, but it's already feeling better."

I nodded and slowly stood. When I was almost to my full height, I lost my balance and almost fell right on Karson.

Oh, God . . .

He caught me around the waist and steadied me. So there we were, me looking down at him in the chair, his hands on my hips, both of us not moving.

I snapped out of his hypnotic gaze and shook my head. "Crap. I'm so sorry!"

He chuckled, and it was the first time I'd seen him smile genuinely. "Don't worry about it."

I looked down at his broken hand. "I hope that didn't hurt you."

Staring at me, he slowly shook his head.

After clearing my throat, I said, "Well, would you like to go see one of the witches, or would you like to wait it out and see if your memories come back on their own?"

He stood up, so now he was towering over me. "I want to do something about this now. Otherwise, I'd rather just leave this town. I don't feel like I have a reason to be here."

"Very well. Since you know where City Hall is, go around the back to a metal door, then go downstairs and you'll find Addie Beaumont. She'll help you." I went around my desk and began to sit to finish up my paperwork.

"No."

I froze mid-sit and cocked my head to the side. "Excuse me?"

"You're coming with me."

I laughed and sat down. "I have to work."

He looked at his watch. "When do you get off work?"

"When I finish," I quipped.

Karson sat back in the chair. "Then I'll wait. Or if you want, I can help."

"No, you can't," I replied, biting back a smile. Not that I would protest having this gorgeous specimen sitting in my chair for the next couple of hours, but there was no way I'd get any work done when all I wanted to do was go sit in his lap and run my fingers over his full lips.

"I appreciate the help, but I have a few more patients to see, plus I'm on call for the ER. So unless you're a medical professional moonlighting as a tattoo artist, I doubt you could be of much help. If you want to wait in the waiting room, there are TVs in there."

He stood up. "Your shift ends at what time?"

Being specific, very smart. "Four."

"I'll see you at four, in the waiting room."

CHAPTER 11

KARSON

I glanced at my watch: 3:58 p.m. The TVs had definitely helped pass the time. I ate a protein bar from the vending machine and drank a bottle of water while I waited. I was still starving, though. I also realized that four p.m. would indicate exactly thirty-eight hours since I arrived in town. I was excited to meet this witch Addie and hoped she could give me some answers.

I also kinda wanted to find the dumb nurse who'd mixed up the meds and throttle her. My brain was still foggy, but I was grateful the irrational anger I felt earlier had subsided. I had no business being pissed off at Scottlin for having a boyfriend. It was none of my business, even if I did feel like she had been flirting a little with me in her office earlier.

Not that I minded.

She was so beautiful, I had no doubt she had a few guys chasing her. I didn't need to be another one. I had enough crap to deal with anyway. I pulled out my phone and scrolled through it, not that I got very far with the crappy signal.

"Hi."

I looked up to see Scottlin standing there in her green scrubs and furry coat. She plunked a knit hat on her head, and in her hand she held a puffy black nylon jacket. She thrust it at me. "Here."

I stood up and stared at it. "Whose is that?"

"Yours, now."

I didn't take it. "Okay, but where did you get it?"

"Lost and found, unclaimed six months. Look at it—it's barely been worn."

I dragged my gaze away from her bright blue eyes and down to the jacket. It really did look new. Shrugging, I took it from her and put it on. Perfect fit. And very warm. "Thank you."

"There are gloves, too. If you want, we can go find you a pair."

I shook my head. "Nah. I'll use the pockets. Besides, I could only wear one anyway." I held up my cast.

She shook two hand warmer pouches to activate them, and slipped them into the pockets of my jacket. Her closeness made me squirm a little—in a good way.

"Those will keep your hands warm."

"Why are you being so nice to me?" I asked, smirking down at her.

She lifted one shoulder. "Because I like you." She began to walk toward the front doors of the hospital and out of the ER.

I followed her. "You think I'm gonna sue you for the meds mix-up, and are just trying to stay on my good side, aren't you?"

She tipped her head back and laughed, her breath coming out in foggy clouds in the cold air. "No. That just goes to show you how much you need your memories. The Court of the Sun and the Moon doesn't entertain such petty and frivolous lawsuits."

Wow. "You're shitting me. And misdosing someone isn't petty."

She stopped walking when we reached a small red Honda. She disarmed it with a beep. I used my good hand to open the driver door for her.

She stood in the open door and said, "When there's magic involved, it changes the game. Thank you for opening my door." She paused and stared up at me. "Now get in."

I didn't have to be told twice. As I sat down, she started up the engine and hit a bunch of buttons to turn on the seat warmers and heat.

She flipped on some classic rock, which made me happy, then

began driving slowly down salted but icy streets until we reached City Hall. She hummed along to "Love Bites" by Def Leppard, which made me smile.

She parked in the back, and we both got out. After walking down a short path, we came upon that same plain gray door we had used to go to Jalen's hearing. It looked like some kind of maintenance entrance. Once inside, we immediately descended the steep flight of stairs that led to the courtroom.

As I was sitting in the ER waiting room, it had suddenly hit me that Scottlin had to be a witch. I wasn't sure why I had at first thought her human, but she had said only supes could see the patient's true race in the medical records, not to mention her extensive knowledge of magic. And hadn't Gavin mentioned something about her not being fully human, anyway? Argh, my brain was in such a fog. But . . . I knew she wasn't a vampire, shifter, elf or other kind of fae, or a wolf, as those were very easy to spot. That left witch or some variation of it. Maybe she was mixed-race?

Once at the bottom of the stairs, after walking down a long hallway, we were in some kind of small reception area. Scottlin went to the only desk in the room, which was unmanned, and rang a bell sitting on it. As we waited, I looked at Scottlin as she removed her cap and gloves. Hair that had escaped her braids was sticking up in places, and I reached over and smoothed them down for her.

"Thanks," she replied. Her cheeks were already red from the cold, so I wasn't sure if she was blushing or not.

I stared down at her. "You're a witch, aren't you?"

"Scottlin Glover, so nice to see you!"

We both looked over to see a gorgeous woman with multiple tattoos and long light brown hair smiling at us. The tiny diamond stud in her nose glinted under the harsh lights of the windowless office.

"Hi," Scottlin said as they hugged briefly.

The woman turned her attention to me. "Karson. What have you been up to? Happy to be back in Havenwood Falls? Seems like you've been gone forever!"

I shook my head. "Addie, I presume?"

She furrowed her brow. "We went to high school together, Karson . . ." She looked at Scottlin. "What's going on?"

"His memories haven't returned. It's been—"

"Thirty-eight hours," I finished.

Addie adjusted her dark-framed glasses and cocked her head to the side slightly. "Well"—she shrugged—"magic affects everyone differently. That said, there's usually something by now, a glimmer of memory, especially since you grew up here." She smiled. "Why don't you have a seat." She indicated a chair in front of her.

I obeyed, keeping my eye on the witch. I never did trust them very much. I listened as Scottlin explained about the mix-up with the medication, both of them staring at me the whole time.

Addie's brows rose. "It can take time to re-acclimate to our town and the magic. That can be disorienting all on its own. But adding in magic meant for vampires? That's a recipe for a major shitstorm."

Scottlin chewed her lip. "It was an accident, I can assure you. The nurse has been counseled, and she's very sorry. I couldn't get her to stop crying."

I wanted to throttle that nurse a little less now.

"But it's not unfixable. In fact," Addie said, reaching into her pocket and plucking out a small vial of powder, "I think I can fix this right now."

It took all I had not to jump up and scream like the Broncos had just won the Super Bowl.

Addie pulled up another chair and sat directly in front of me. She glanced back at Scottlin and said, "I think once the medication is out of his system completely, his memories will start coming back slowly. I'm just gonna speed that along for him."

"You don't have to talk about me like I'm not here," I commented.

Addie had the grace to look embarrassed. "Sorry. This is a teachable moment for me, so I had my instructor's hat on. I meant nothing by it."

I looked at Scottlin. "So you are a witch."

She nodded. "Half."

I looked at Addie, and she smiled. "Ready?"

"Fuck yes, I'm ready."

Addie chuckled. "Same ol' Karson." She shook some of the shimmery purple powder from the vial into the palm of her hand, then handed the vial to Scottlin. Her smile faded, and she closed her eyes. She began chanting low in what I assumed was Latin, then her eyes popped open. With her hand cupped in front of my face, she pursed her lips and said, "Close your eyes."

I did as I was told, then I heard her blow. I inhaled in surprise as I felt the powder go up my nose and down my throat. I instinctually began to cough and sputter. "Holy shit, that's gross!"

Both women laughed.

I opened my eyes and saw them both standing there, staring expectantly at me. But no magical rush of memories exploded into my brain.

"Well?" Scottlin asked. "Anything?"

"Nope," I replied, as I stood up and swiped my hand over my face, not wanting to be sparkly.

Addie smiled. "Don't worry, it won't be long now."

"What was that, some kind of memory-restoring fairy dust?" I asked.

She laughed. "No, just a spell to clean that stuff out of your system quicker. You may be peeing a lot this evening. Or sweating. Or both."

"Awesome," I murmured.

"What now?" Scottlin asked.

Addie put the vial back into her pocket. "Take him home, let him rest." She looked at me and adjusted her glasses again. "Are you staying with Jalen?"

"Yeah, but he's in jail."

"I know. Because of you."

My eyebrows hit my hairline. "Hey now. I wouldn't go that far. He wrote me the email, not the other way around. I didn't ask to come back here. I was pretty much coerced."

Addie shook her head, frowning. "You shouldn't have left to begin with, Karson. We all told you not to, but you let your pain guide your decision, not your logic. Now you're paying the price for it, aren't you?"

The way she said it didn't seem scolding or rude, but more motherly or sympathetic. "I have no idea what made me leave, but I can't wait to get my memories back to find out."

"Now, that, I wouldn't be too quick to want to remember," Addie said with a grimace.

CHAPTER 12

KARSON

*A*fter thanking Addie, we left City Hall, and Scottlin drove me back to Jalen's house.

I sat in the car for a little bit and looked at Scottlin before I said, "Thank you."

She smiled. "You're welcome. Please let me know if your hand gets worse. You can reach me at the medical center."

I looked at her phone sitting in the middle console. I picked it up and swiped the screen. I went into her contacts and added my name and number, then sent myself a text.

She said nothing, just watched the interaction curiously. I felt my phone vibrate in my pocket before I said, "I'll text you."

Scottlin laughed. "Well, okay then. A guy who takes charge. Nice."

I bit back a smile and resisted the urge to finger her hair. "Like that, do you?"

She pursed her lips together, and I wanted to kiss them. "Get out of here, and get some rest. Oh, and please let me know if your memories return?"

"I will." I still longed to touch her, but decided I'd better not. Her hands were still gloved, so kissing one wouldn't have had the same effect. "Drive safely."

"Thank you."

I got out of the car and watched her drive off before carefully making my way up the icy path toward the front door. Looking up into the darkening sky, I could see snow clouds begin to move in. I sort of hated this time of year. January always seemed to be the darkest. Dark when you got up, and dark when you got home.

With a sigh, I opened the front door, which had not been locked, and was hit with the smell of pot. After hanging my coat on a hall tree in the entryway, I went into the kitchen.

Gavin came waltzing in with a joint in his hand. He looked at me expectantly, then slowly asked, "Where you been, man?"

"At the hospital, mostly. Went to see Jalen, too."

"How is he?" Gavin asked, before bringing the joint up to his lips and taking a long drag.

I looked at it, then him. "Not happy."

Gavin chuckled, then choked on the smoke. "Shit." He coughed some more. "You want some?" He held it out to me.

I rarely touched the stuff, but my hand was starting to throb again. "Sure."

I took a drag from it and held the smoke in while I stared at my cousin through the haze.

Gavin grabbed a glass from the cabinet and filled it with tap water. After taking a long drink, he said, "You remember me yet?"

I shook my head and blew the smoke out of the side of my mouth. "Nope."

"What the fuck, man." He finished the water and set the glass in the sink. "I think we need to take you to see Addie."

I handed him back the blunt. "Already done. The cutie from the hospital took me down there."

"Who? The redhead?"

I simply nodded. Then I went into my day and told him everything, the drug relaxing me and making me chatty, like a chick.

The joint had been discarded, and he now stood with his arms folded over his chest. "That's a trip. Maybe we should go see your dad. Might stir something up?" He pointed to my head.

My brow furrowed. "It might, but I don't remember my parents at all, still."

Gavin frowned. "True. It's just your dad, though. Not your mom."

"Where is she?"

He raked his long fingers through his white-blond hair and shook his head. "We'll talk about that later. Hopefully, I won't have to, though."

This was the second cryptic thing I'd heard about something unpleasant regarding my past, and yet, I couldn't wait to remember what it was.

I think.

"Probably not a good idea to see my dad if I can't remember him. Might make it weird. Don't you think?"

Gavin nodded. "You're probably right. Let's order pizza and play some Fortnite."

"Yes to the pizza. Not sure about Fortnite. Isn't that for kids?"

He chuckled. "Nah, it's fun, c'mon." He ordered the pizza while I set up the game.

We played for hours, until we couldn't keep our eyes open any longer.

"Kar-Kar, you know Mommy has to go. You don't need to cry every fuckin' time," she slurred.

"What the hell, Lyn. He's only ten. Stop talking to him like that." I heard my dad's voice, but did not look up from where I was curled into a ball in the corner of my room.

"I'm not crying!" I gritted out, with my head still tucked down so my dad couldn't see my bloody nose. I had toilet paper stuffed in my nostrils, and I probably sounded like I was crying. But I wasn't.

"Whatever," my mom said, then blew smoke through her mouth. The smell made me queasy. "I'm outta here. You deal with your stupid-ass kid."

I heard the front door slam before slowly looking up. Dad's massive frame took up the doorway to my room. He looked at me sympathetically and said, "I'm sorry, kid. She really is a useless mother."

His words stung. My little heart and brain couldn't understand why I was angry at him for saying bad things about Mom. She had just backhanded me so hard, I had flown across the room, landing on my video game console. My back ached where the corner of it had dug into my skin and muscle.

I stood up and shrugged, not knowing what to say.

Dad came toward me. I looked up at his thinning blond hair and into eyes so much like mine. "Let's go get some burgers."

I pulled the toilet paper out of my nose and threw it onto the floor. "I'm not hungry."

"Yet you're going to go with me, anyway. We'll go to Burger Bar. I know you love their milkshakes."

He was right; I loved them. I went into the bathroom attached to my room and said, "Where did Mom go?"

I heard him audibly sigh. "I don't know, kid."

Now I wanted to cry. "Is she coming back?"

"Eventually. She always does. Now wash that blood off your face and get your shoes on."

I blinked my eyes open, and everything was blurry. Wet tears slid down my face and into my ears. I sat up and looked around the room. It was the exact same one from my dream—just the furniture was different.

God, I hated my mom. That bitch . . . I was so glad she was dead.

Whoa! Oh, my God . . . "Oh, my God!"

My mom. Chasing that next high, she'd died taking mushrooms especially poisonous to our kind two years ago, right here in this house. My dad was devastated. I couldn't handle it. More tears sprang to my eyes.

"I'm the one who found her," I said to no one in particular. The pain in my chest slammed into me with the same savagery it had two years ago. I put my good hand over it and closed my eyes, trying to stay the pain and battle back emotion. Damn, remembering kinda sucked. I took a deep breath and closed my eyes, willing the agony away.

Screw crying over her.

I threw back the covers, flew out of my room, and went downstairs. It was quiet. I glanced at the clock on the microwave: 5:52 a.m. Too early to knock on Gavin's door with the good news. I went back upstairs, used the bathroom, and sat back on the bed in my room. I picked up my phone and texted the only person I could think of—Scottlin.

Me: I remember!

I set the phone down and let my memories flood in. Going to high school with Gavin and Addie. God, I had such a crush on her back then. Everyone else had crushed on her BFF Michaela Petran, but I'd thought Addie was way cuter. Finding my mom on the bathroom floor in a pool of her own mushroom-filled vomit. Me trying to rouse her. Screaming at her to wake up. Slapping her in desperation. Yelling for Dad. Jalen and Gavin coming running. Rushing her to the HFMC, blinded by tears.

But it had been too late.

Anger and sadness invaded my heart. I looked down at my arms, and it was no longer a mystery why I had all those circular burn marks all over them. The tattoos covered them up just fine, but I shouldn't have had to sleeve my arms and tattoo my chest just so I wouldn't have to look at them. I should have been able to get the tattoos for art expression, not memory suppression.

I pushed my mother from my mind and immediately wanted to go see my dad. I *ached* to see him. I shouldn't have left him the way I did. But at the time, I just had to leave. I distinctly remember feeling like the box canyon town was literally closing in all around me, trying to suffocate me, coffin me.

I looked around the room and had to think hard for a minute as to why Jalen and Gavin were living in the house I grew up in, and not my dad. He had been living here when I left. Things must have changed.

My phone chimed.

Scottlin: That's amazing! I'm so happy for you.

Me: Sorry if I woke you, I had to tell someone, lol

Since there was no way I was going back to sleep, I got up and went into the bathroom for a shower. My phone buzzed again.

Scottlin: You didn't. I'm already at work. Came in early to get paperwork done. Somebody distracted me yesterday ;)

I grinned at her flirtation and then stripped out of my T-shirt and shorts. I went to text her back, my fingers hovering over the phone.

Fuck it.

Me: Can I take you out somewhere tonight to celebrate?

I started up the shower and waited for it to get hot. And for her to text back before I got in. *Buzz.*

Scottlin: That would be great. Burger Bar?

Me: Sounds perfect. What time you off?

Scottlin: 4 again

Me: See you there at 5. I would pick you up, but . . . you know

Scottlin: LOL yes I know. Do you need a ride?

Me: Nah, I'll manage

Scottlin: Have a good day

Me: You too

I was smiling like a jackass all throughout my shower. I got my memories back, I was gonna get to see my dad today, and I had a date with a hottie tonight. It was going to be a great day.

CHAPTER 13

KARSON

"*G*avin Fuckhead Kane, birthday July second. Loves shopping, gaming, and vampires. Gay as fuck."

He chuckled as he strolled into the kitchen, looking down at his phone. He lifted his eyes to me. "Memories returned, I see, asswipe?"

"Yep," I replied, before spooning more Froot Loops into my face.

"Fuckhead isn't my given middle name, you know," he replied facetiously, checking his hair in the reflection of the microwave door.

"Well, we gave it to you. And we've been calling you that for so long, I can't remember your real one."

"Henry," he replied with an eye roll. He went to the fridge, pulled out a box of orange juice, and splashed some into a cup.

I looked at his pressed khaki pants, his sweater over a collared shirt, and his shiny shoes. "Where you headed?"

"Time to go back to Denver. I only stay here a day or two a month, so I don't forget this place, then leave."

"That's right," I murmured.

"Yep. Anyway, got a meeting later with my boss. Plus, I miss Beckett."

I wrinkled my nose. "You still dating that vampire?"

"Yes, asshole."

I laughed. "Okay, well, good thing I got my memories back before you left."

"Yes, thank the gods. You were working my last nerve." He grabbed the keys to his little Nissan sports car and headed toward the front door.

"Hey, before you go, why are you and Jalen living in my house? Where's my dad?"

"Oh, I just stay here when I come back to town. Jalen moved in when his dad went to prison. Hasn't moved out yet. Your dad remarried and is living near the falls with a witch named Regina."

I lifted an eyebrow. "Seriously?"

"Yep, his address and phone number's on the fridge. He lets Jalen stay here as long as he pays the utilities and keeps the house and yard up."

"I have more questions, but I'll get them out of Dad. I'll see you later, I guess?"

He opened the front door and moved his backpack to his other shoulder. "Will I? Or are you going to leave again?"

I lifted a shoulder. "Not sure, but I doubt it. Don't have much in the Springs except a job and a crappy apartment. I don't even have a car."

He smiled and clapped me on the shoulder. "Good decision. Take care."

I gave him a quick man-hug and lightly pounded him on the back. "Be safe."

Gavin nodded and walked down the two front steps and toward his car. After he'd driven off, I closed the front door and went to the fridge to find my dad's info. I found the paper easily enough and pulled out my cell phone. Shit, did this town have Uber yet? Guess I was about to find out . . .

I pulled up the app, waited for it to find my location, and waited some more. Then I imputed the address from the paper. It took a good three or four minutes, but I finally got notified that my driver was on his way.

"Jakeel in a"—I put my face closer to the screen and blinked—

"1999 orange Lincoln Town Car? Huh. Didn't know they came in orange." Then I glanced at the app again to see it wasn't Uber at all, but something called "Luber."

Where had that app come from . . . ?

I went back up the stairs to my room and opened my closet door. Inside was a dresser where I knew I had warm gloves and hats. I also remembered leaving a wad of cash in there, having cursed myself for leaving it when I was halfway down the mountain the last time; I'd been too stubborn to go back for it. I skipped the gloves since I could only wear one, found a warm scarf and set it on top of the dresser, then opened the bottom drawer and felt around for an envelope taped to the top of the inside of the drawer. My fingers located it.

Yes!

I opened up the envelope, and the two thousand dollars I'd left there was all still intact. God, if I had known this was here, I'd have a working car right now. I remembered I had stormed off with about that much in my bank account, but it had dwindled quickly.

My phone buzzed in my pocket, so I pulled it out and looked at the screen: **Your driver is arriving.**

I shut the drawer and closet, threw the scarf on, and pounded down the stairs while shoving the envelope into my pocket. After grabbing the black coat Scottlin had given me (I liked it better than the wool one I knew was inside the hall closet where we kept the coats), I flipped the curtain back to see an orange hearse idling in front of the house.

What in the . . .

My phone rang with a strange number. "Hello?"

"Karson?" said a man's voice, which was a little on the high side.

"Yeah?"

"This is Jakeel. I'm your Luber driver. I'm out front, pal."

I tilted my head to the side and looked at the orange monstrosity. "In a hearse?"

"Yes, sirree. See you soon." He hung up.

I shook my head and went outside, leaving the door unlocked

because I hadn't had time to go dig for a house key. Slipping into the backseat, I noted it was nice and warm in the car.

"Hey," I said to the driver.

"Howdy," he replied cheerily as he used the old gear-lever-type shifter to put the car into drive. He was a tiny man with about four strands of hair combed over his bald head. He had an unlit cigar between his lips, which were covered on top by a thick, brown mustache. The cold gray day did nothing to dull the sparkle of his green and red Christmas sweater.

"So this is quite a bit a ways out from here," he replied, pointing with heavily jeweled fingers to the map on his smartphone, which I noticed was mounted on some kind of contraption that looked like it was built from beige PVC piping. It was bolted to the dash and floor, and double-sided Velcro tape held the phone to the top of it.

"That's fine. I'll pay whatever," I replied quietly as I watched the car leave my neighborhood. "I just don't have my own car, obviously."

He chuckled. "That's no problemo. I'm the only Luber driver in the town, so you're stuck with me if ya need a ride-o back. So, are ya a newbie in town?"

I bit back a smile. "Nah, I'm from here. Just got back."

"That's super duper! Are you enjoying being back?"

Oh, geez. I wondered if he'd stop if I gave one-word answers. But I was probably stuck using him for a ride back later, so I'd better be nice. "Yep, it's good to be home."

He smiled at me through the rearview mirror. "I bet it's awesome-sauce! I love Havenwood Falls."

He turned a knob on the radio and began to sing along to "Bohemian Rhapsody" by Queen. I just chuckled and sat back while I watched the scenery go by. We walked down the main street, and I smiled at all the familiar shops and restaurants. I couldn't wait for that milkshake tonight at Burger Bar.

CHAPTER 14

KARSON

*T*he hearse's tires crunched over gravel after we turned off the main highway. I stared at the nearly frozen waterfalls trickling down the mountain to my left. They emptied into the Mathews River below, and memories of playing and fishing in that river when I was younger brought a smile to my lips. I also had especially fond memories of going to the Paddle Fest every year; it had been my favorite part of summer. My dad had taken me several times. My mother, of course, was never there.

I shoved her out of my mind and looked up when the car came to a stop. I briefly wondered if I should have called first, but I wanted to surprise Dad.

"Okeydokey, we're here, Karson."

In front of the car sat a cozy, quaint-looking house with ivy crawling up its walls and smoke billowing out of its chimney stack. A cobblestone path led to a big wooden front door with a gnome's head as a knocker. A large RV and small SUV beside it.

I handed Jakeel a five-dollar tip and thanked him. "I may need a ride back. I'll let you know."

"Sounds swell. You take care now. Toodle-oo!"

As I went to exit the car, I noticed Jakeel was sitting on what could only be described as a child's booster seat. He had some kind of special pedals that stuck up really far from the floor so he could reach them. He was tiny, like a little person. He was so odd, I couldn't quite tell if he was human or something else.

I closed the car door behind me and walked slowly up the cobblestone path. *God, I hope somebody's home, or I'm stuck.*

I used the door knocker and pounded three times. My eyes widened as I spied a planter box full of peonies. I never saw them in winter. I carefully plucked one and quickly popped it into my mouth. "Thank you, witches. Mmmm."

Now shifting from foot to foot for warmth, I didn't have to wait long until the door opened slowly and a middle-aged woman stood there. She was pretty, with curly blond hair and a friendly smile. She held a dishcloth in her hands and was drying them on it. "Hi, can I help you?"

I swallowed the flower. "Uh, is Ellis Kane here?"

She furrowed her brow, then her eyes went wide. "Karson?"

I nodded. "Yes."

She opened the door wider to let me in, and beamed from ear to ear. "Oh, my goddess. Ellis is gonna freak out." She hugged me. It was awkward because I didn't know her.

"Ellis!" she yelled, after she broke the hug. Seeing my face, she said, "I'm sorry. I'm Regina. Your dad's wife. I like tea, photography, gardening, and awkward hugging."

I chuckled. "Nice to meet you."

"What, woman? I'm not done fixing—"

I turned around when I heard my dad's voice. His eyes went wide. He dropped the wrench from his hand, immediately rushed over to me, and wrapped his huge arms around me. "Karson. Son. I'm so fuckin' happy to see you!"

"Language, Ellis," Regina corrected with a grin. "I'll make some tea."

I looked up at him, and the only thing I could think to say was, "I'm so sorry, Dad."

He shook his head. I could see his face had gained more lines, and more silvery threads had popped up along his temples. Otherwise, he looked exactly the same. "No, I'm sorry. I shouldn't have fallen apart like that when your mom died. I should have been stronger for you."

"It's okay. It was immature, me leaving like that. I won't do that again."

He put his arm around me and led me to a quaint dining room. He indicated for me to sit. I took off my jacket and scarf and set them on one of the chairs before doing so.

Dad sat next to me right as Regina arrived with steaming cups of tea. I wasn't a tea drinker, but the warmth looked inviting.

"Where have you been?" was his first question.

"Colorado Springs."

"What do you do there?" he asked, lifting the tea to his lips.

"Tattoo artist."

"Figured. You make a decent living?"

I nodded. "I do okay."

"What brought you back here? Surely, you couldn't remember this place. How did you get back?"

"Jalen," I said. "Sent me an email that sounded really weird at the time. I followed my gut and took a bus to Montrose, then boarded the Havenwood Falls bus here. Got in almost three days ago."

"Okay, first off . . . three days ago? Why didn't you come see me sooner? And those little shits didn't even call?"

"Just got my memories back this morning."

I launched into the story, and knowing Regina was a witch, I wouldn't have to hide anything.

"Addie fixes everything." Regina smiled.

"The hell happened to your hand?" Dad asked.

I looked down at it. "Well, the oven door might need replacing." I grinned sheepishly. "I sorta punched it and broke it."

"Kid, you have got to learn to control that temper."

"I know," I murmured.

"Now, how did Jalen send you an email about this place and not get his chops busted by the Court?"

"Well, about that. And why he didn't call you. He's, uh, in jail."

Dad raked his fingers through his hair. "Shit."

"We need to help him. He risked his neck for me. He said Uncle Will gets out of prison soon and he needed my help. Why would he need my help?"

"My brother is a hothead, like you. Just don't use your affliction on people. Almost killed that guy, he did."

"I know. I remember that. I'm surprised he's getting out at all."

"He's lucky the guy didn't die, really. But in the big picture, it wasn't intentional. Will was just pissed."

I nodded. "What now?"

"Before I answer that, are you back? Like, to stay?"

"Yes," I replied. "I got nothing there I can't leave behind. My car don't even work."

"That sucks," he replied, chuckling. "So you need a vehicle, then?"

"Yes, I had to Uber here. I mean, Luber."

"What the hell is Luber?"

"Like a taxi," I came back, laughing.

He got up and went to a keyholder mounted to the wall and plucked up a set. He tossed them at me. "You can have the Harley. And stay at the house. There's a spare house key on that ring, too. Just get yourself a job soon, 'cause it don't look like Jalen can pay the utilities and shit right now."

My face lit up. "Thanks, Dad. Where's the bike?"

He jutted a thumb behind him. "In the shed out back."

"But . . . I don't have a motorcycle license. Just a regular one."

Dad chuckled. "Sheriff K don't give a shit. You just gotta watch out for Deputy Conall."

I smiled. "That's true."

Regina asked if I wanted more tea, and I shook my head.

"Let's go see the bike," I said excitedly, standing up.

Dad grinned and set his teacup down. He'd had the Harley for at least ten years and never rode it. And judging from the crossover SUV and the RV parked out front, I doubted the thing had seen road in a while.

We exited through the back door of the kitchen, with Regina fussing at us to put on our coats. We quickly shrugged them on and walked a small garden path to a large tool shed that was almost as big as my studio apartment back in the Springs.

Dad produced a key from the pocket of his work pants and used it to unlock the padlock holding the door secure. He opened the doors, and I peered inside, squinting in the darkness before Dad flipped a light switch.

"Fancy," I said, then whistled through my teeth. The shed had epoxy-painted floors, fully finished and painted walls, and electricity.

He laughed. "Regina calls it my man cave."

"It totally is one. I'm a bit jealous."

He made a scoffing noise. "You and Jalen got that whole house with a garage back home. Make your own man cave."

I looked at my dad's amused eyes. "I just might." I glanced around to see tools neatly hung on a board against one wall and a lawnmower in the corner. "What, no bathroom?"

"I ain't no plumber," he replied.

That was true. He was a mechanic who dabbled in residential electrical work and carpentry. He sometimes subcontracted for McCabe & Sons Construction.

I went over to the bike and pulled the sheet off it. My eyes went wide. The 2008 Harley Nightster glinted under the overhead lights. "Dad, this thing looks brand new."

He grunted. "That's because it practically is. I think I've ridden her a dozen times, maybe. She'd just be collectin' dust if I left her in here. She's yours."

Holy shit!

CHAPTER 15

SCOTTLIN

I replaced the cap on the lip gloss and checked my reflection one last time. With my hair down, it was kind of wild, and I always felt like Carrot Top because I could never control its unruly curls.

"It's just burgers, Scottlin. Calm down," I said to my reflection.

I resisted the urge to pull my hair back into some kind of clip or braid, but instead pushed it all behind me so it cascaded down my back. I finished applying some mascara and blush, then threw the makeup back into the drawer in my bathroom. I quickly spritzed some body spray on and then checked my phone: 4:42 p.m.

The drive to Burger Bar was only five minutes. Should I be early?

God, why am I so nervous?

I blew out a breath and went into the living room of my small apartment. I located my knee-high boots quickly enough and slipped them on. After smoothing down my flowery black shirt and making sure my jeans didn't have anything on them, I shrugged on my jacket and threw on a scarf.

On the car ride over, I had to tell myself to just chill. There was no reason to be this anxious. I wasn't this nervous when I went on my first date with Len. *So what gives?* Probably because Karson was twice as hot as Len. I giggled to myself. That was most definitely true.

When I arrived, I saw Karson in the parking lot, sitting on a shiny black-and-silver motorcycle in blue jeans, a dark-colored tee, and a black leather jacket. Did he just buy that motorcycle today?

Who cares? He looked smoking on it.

He glanced up from where he'd been looking at his phone and smiled when he saw me pull in.

I parked and killed the engine, but before I could exit the car, he had my door open and a hand out. I glanced down at it, then him, then put my hand in his.

He hoisted me up and then closed the door for me. "Lock it," he instructed.

So bossy. I laughed and hit the fob to create the satisfying beep. "Happy?" I asked with a smirk.

"I am now," he said, looking down at me.

Karson placed his hand on the small of my back and ushered me toward the front door of Burger Bar. He opened the door for me, and we waited in line at the counter to order. It smelled delicious in here. My stomach somersaulted with hunger.

I was really beginning to like what I saw in Karson. Despite his tough exterior, he really did behave like a gentleman. I was anxious to see what else he was going to impress me with.

We both decided on bacon burgers and shakes, then found a table to wait for our orders. It wasn't long until Shayna Collins, a girl who worked with me at the hospital, but also worked here waitressing part time, skated over to us and set our trays down in front of us.

"Anything else?" she asked.

"Nope, looks good," Karson replied.

She winked at him, then looked at me before skating off. "Enjoy your dinner, doc."

Karson looked at me. "You know her?"

"Yeah, she works at the hospital."

"She always call you doc?"

"All non-medical staff call everyone in a white lab coat that," I replied, amused.

He laughed and unwrapped his straw. "I see."

"New bike?" I grabbed a fry and used it to point toward the windows, where night was beginning to descend, the parking lot lights popping on one by one.

He picked up his burger with his good hand, then pierced me with his intense stormy gaze. "Yes and no. Dad's had it ten years and never rides it, so he gave it to me today when I went to see him."

My eyes went wide. "Really? Wow. That was super cool of him."

He grinned. "Yes, it was. I'm having the best day I've had in two years."

I tilted my head to the side. "Yeah? Why's that?"

"Because I woke up with my memories—not all of them good, but that's a story for another time. Then I got to see my dad for the first time in forever, and meet his cool new wifey. Then he gave me a Harley. A fuckin' Harley, Scottlin. I had always been envious of that bike, and he had never let me ride it, except one time. Now it's mine!"

I loved the excitement on his face and in his voice. He was so damned cute.

"And to top off my day, I have a date with the most gorgeous girl in Havenwood Falls."

My eyebrows practically hit my hairline. I absentmindedly began playing with my hair as I felt heat creep into my cheeks. Compliments were hard for me to accept, but I could never figure out why. "I . . . I . . . Uh, thank you." I managed a smile.

His gaze roamed my face and head, and he pointed at my hair. "I like the curls. Why do you always wear those braids?"

I shrugged. "It gets in my way at work. And when I'm not at work, I'll end up messing with it. Easier to keep it tamed, I guess."

He chuckled and pointed at my right index finger, which had a strand twisted around it. "Like that?"

I immediately put my hands into my lap, chagrined. "Yes, like that."

He laughed and bit into his bacon cheeseburger.

"So, besides riding around on your Harley, what do you plan to do while you're in town?" I asked.

He set his burger down. "I'm not 'in town.' I live here."

I lifted an eyebrow and bit back a grin. "Really? You're staying?"

He nodded. "Oh, yeah. I should have never left."

This excited me way more than it should have. I slid some hair behind my ear. "I'm very happy to hear that."

"Yeah? Why's that?" he asked with a mischievous glint in his eye.

"You guys still good?" Shayna asked, seeming to show up out of nowhere.

We both replied in the affirmative, and she skated off.

I wasn't sure how to answer Karson's question, so I shoveled a French fry into my mouth to avoid it. Goddess, this place had amazing food. Then I made sure the bacon was crispy before I lifted the burger and bit into it. I had to resist the urge to let my eyes roll back in my head.

After I set the burger down, I heard chuckling.

I looked up to see Karson touching his chin. "You have a little . . ."

Mortified, I quickly wiped my face on the paper napkin. *I suck at dating!* "Thanks. There's no ladylike way to eat a burger here, it seems."

He took a long pull from the straw of his milkshake and said, "I don't expect ladylike behavior while eating bacon cheeseburgers. Nobody here does."

I asked him a question I knew I might regret, but I was feeling kind of empowered at the moment. "And when do you expect ladylike behavior?"

His burger paused at his lips, then he set it back into the basket. After a quick glance around the quickly crowding restaurant, he pierced me with a smoky look. "Not in the bedroom, either, if that's what you meant."

I pursed my lips to keep from grinning and simply nodded. "Duly noted, sir."

"Don't call me sir. Not in public, anyway."

Thinking the conversation was bordering on inappropriate, but secretly loving it, I decided we could continue it later. So I changed the subject. "Tell me about your past."

He bit into his burger and chewed a bit before swallowing. I did the same, patiently waiting.

"What do you want to know?" he asked after swallowing.

I daintily wiped my lips with the napkin before staring at him across the table. "Pretty much everything."

CHAPTER 16

KARSON

*W*hat was I going to tell her? I wasn't sure. I was too distracted by the mass of red curls lying on her breasts and the way her cherry-red lips moved when she spoke. How was I supposed to concentrate on anything she had asked?

To keep from getting too aroused in the restaurant, I began to talk. "Uh. Okay. Well, I was born here. Went to school here. Graduated from HFHS six years ago. Worked right out of high school at HF Ink. Rowdy's an amazing teacher."

"I remember that place," Scottlin replied. "But he closed up shop a couple of years ago."

This surprised me—that would have been right after I left—but I didn't say anything.

"So you already had some kind of artistic talent before you started tattooing?"

I nodded. "Yes. I used to draw and sketch to pass the time while I was . . ." *Locked in a room with no food or water for days.* "Bored."

Scottlin smiled, and it was beautiful. She only knew the good, not the bad. And I would keep it that way. Her pretty smile made me happy, and encouraged me to keep going.

"Anyway, Rowdy must have seen a talent in me of some kind, because he taught me everything I know about tattooing. How the ink worked. How to keep a steady hand. How to talk to clients. Everything."

"He did beautiful work," Scottlin agreed. "Did he do any of yours?"

"My first one. It's on my calf. I'll show you later." I winked at her.

She grinned and cleared her throat. "I only have the butterfly." She held out her wrist. "Because they made me, of course. It's sorta for my dad. He died when I was a baby. Or so I'm told."

This interested me. "You don't know?"

"My mom said he died on the pass out of town. Snowy day on his motorcycle. He was human, so I believe it's possible."

That answered the question I was going to ask anyway. I lowered my voice. "So your mom's a witch, and your dad was human?"

She nodded. "Yep."

I swirled my fry in the ketchup on my plate. "Do you have full witch powers?"

She shook her head. "No. But my mother is a healer, and I have been blessed with that gift. When a case comes into the hospital, and I can't diagnose it, I cheat a little and use magic to find out what's wrong. Other than that, and having the advantages supes have around here, that's it for me."

I was impressed. "Well, that's a cool superpower to have."

Just then, the bell above the door chimed, and three pale men dressed in black clothing walked in.

I watched closely as they didn't order any food, but took a booth near the back. They eyeballed me as they walked past.

"What?" Scottlin asked as I met her stare once more.

"Nothing," I murmured, biting my tongue.

She glanced back at the group, then to me. "They're no more vampire by choice than you are elven. Ignore them. I do."

"See, that's where you're wrong. They chose to become that." I jabbed my thumb behind me toward where they sat.

Scottlin shook her head and smiled tightly at me. "No, some of them didn't. They were born that way."

I knew this. The moroi . . . they were literally born into that life, and I had no problem with them. But the ones seated in the back of Burger Bar weren't them. They were the ones who had *chosen* to be turned.

"I know," I said. "But not them."

"Just don't stare," she commented. Then her face darkened. "They have bad tempers."

I looked into her eyes. "You know them?"

"One. Treated him when he was first turned. He didn't know what was happening and came to the ER."

My eyebrows hit my hairline. "Some vamp turned him without his permission and then left him on his own?"

"Oh, yeah. The Court took care of him."

"Good," I said, finishing up the last of my burger. We changed the subject and chatted some more about anything and everything.

After a few more minutes, I asked, "Are you ready to go?"

She nodded, and we got up to leave. I noticed the vampires weren't in the restaurant any longer and wondered how they'd snuck out without me noticing. This was why I didn't care for them. Much too slippery.

I held open the door for her, and we made our way outside. I wasn't sure where we would go next, but I didn't want our date to end. I looked up to see the vampires hovering around my bike. "Shit."

Scottlin glanced up at me, then to where I was looking. "What are they doing?"

"Stay here," I told her, as we were still in front of the restaurant under the lights.

I strode purposefully toward them, and they looked up when they saw me approach.

"This yours?" one asked, a smirk on his pasty face. He was tall and thin with black hair and thick sideburns.

Let's try polite first. "Yeah. I'm gonna need you to move so I can leave, though."

"Where did you get this?" another one asked. He was shorter and thicker than the other, with long blond hair tied back into a ponytail.

"None of your business. Now move. *Please.*"

"No," the taller one said. "Can't we take her for a little test drive? Been in the market for a Harley, and this is just perfect."

"It's not for fucking sale." I put my hands on my hips and began to concentrate on the magic inside me. I could feel my chest growing warm, and my head was starting to float with anger.

The tall one slung his leg over the seat and sat down. He stroked the handlebar like a lover. "Oh, come on. How much you want for it?"

I slowly walked toward them and got within six feet of the bike. I couldn't take on three vampires by myself, but I could make them hurt. I looked at the one sitting on my bike right in the eye and pushed all the rage and magic out of me, delivering a sting to his brain.

"Dammit!" He put his hands to his head and doubled over.

Using his weakness to my advantage, I yanked him by the coat and tossed him onto the ground of the parking lot.

He quickly rose up onto his knees, cradling his head.

I turned and looked at the other two, who were staring in horror at their friend, and looking confused.

"Fucking elves!" the vamp said, still gripping his head.

The magic still poured out of me, aimed right at him. "It'll stop once you're a good distance away. Now get the fuck outta here before it spreads to the rest of your undead body."

The two picked up their friend, and the three rushed off at vampire speed. I hoped someone in the restaurant would tell the Court they'd used supernatural speed in front of humans.

Scottlin came over and put her hand on my arm. "Are you all right?"

I looked down into her pretty face and instantly relaxed. "Yeah, I'm fine."

"Let's get out of here." She went toward her car. "Follow me."

I got on my bike, started it up, and followed her out of the parking lot.

~

She coasted into the parking lot of the Annex, where movies were shown the second Saturday of every month during the winters. *But wait, it's like Wednesday.* I pulled up next to her and killed the engine to my bike. After putting the kickstand down, I went over and opened her door for her.

Love Bites by Def Leppard was blasting out of the speakers again, and she looked at me sheepishly and turned it down. "Oops."

"You've got that song on repeat, or what?" I teased.

She shut off the engine and just smiled in acknowledgement as she went to get out.

"I haven't seen a movie in forever," I said as I helped her out of the car. "But they don't show movies here on Wednesdays."

She nodded as I closed her door. "There's a special screening tonight. I heard some patients talking today about it. I hope this is okay? It's too cold to do anything else."

"I agree." I grabbed her hand as we walked toward the entrance. The place was brimming with people, and I didn't care who saw us holding hands. She squeezed mine when we reached the front and saw people staring at us.

We approached the small ticket booth and I looked at the sign.

"Hmm. Looks like they're showing *Death Race Four*. Is that okay?" She looked up at me.

I chuckled. "Uh, yeah, but it's not like we have a choice. You sure you wanna see that?"

"Why not?" She smiled. "I really liked the first three."

I bought us tickets for the show, and once we were seated, we had about twenty minutes to kill.

She looked over at me and said, "So how often do you have to use your, uh"—she glanced around briefly and lowered her voice—"superpower?"

CHAPTER 17

SCOTTLIN

*I*t was a legitimate question, but he was staring at me like I had two heads.

I bit back a smile. "What?"

He licked his lips and looked around the theater. There wasn't anyone seated on either side of us, but there were people in front of us.

"To answer your question, not often. Very rarely. I've never used it on a human. Only"—he cleared his throat—"those people."

I nodded.

"I also want you to know that if the guy had been by himself, I wouldn't have used it. I would have just yanked him off and probably beat his ass. But between the hand and the fact that there were three of them, that was the quickest way to give him a healthy dose of respect for . . . my kind."

Made sense. "I hope you don't think I was judging you, I had just never seen a, uh, person of your race use that . . . uh, what's it called?"

"Affliction."

"Well, it's a handy trick," I commented.

"We're only supposed to use it in self-defense, if I'm being honest. So that was just a preemptive strike before the self-defense would have had to come into play. That's how I think of it, anyway."

"I agree," I said, meaning it. "Do you realize your eyes flashed red when you were doing it?"

He nodded. "Yeah. But I'm told if you blink, you'd miss it."

The screen was blank, and people were still filing in and taking seats. I was glad we had some time to talk.

Karson reached over and grabbed my hand with his good one. His touch made me feel warm inside, and the way he pierced me with his intense eyes made my stomach feel like a swarm of butterflies was about to burst up and out through my mouth.

"I'm gonna kiss you."

Right as the lights dimmed in the Annex, I nodded absently as his face closed the distance between us. His beautiful lips that I had been longing to touch finally connected with mine, and all I could see when I closed my eyes were stars shooting from behind my lids. The butterflies increased their speed in my stomach, and something warm and delicious began to blossom even lower.

Then his hand was on my face, his strong fingers stroking my jawline as he cupped my cheek. When his lips moved in perfect sync with mine, I swooned. When he slowly licked the seam of my lips, demanding entry, I felt like I couldn't breathe. When his tongue mingled with mine, I never wanted the moment to end.

Suddenly, the screen flickered to life and exposed us. Reluctantly, Karson broke the kiss. His beautiful lips glimmered under the light from the screen, and I could tell he was trying to catch his breath. I was sure my face reflected the same.

"You . . . you . . . are an incredible kisser," I said breathlessly.

He grinned, and those butterflies picked up speed again when his hand stroked my face. "That wasn't my best performance." He looked around the Annex again. "Audience and all."

I reached up and grabbed a strand of my hair. I just couldn't leave it alone when it was down, and being nervous didn't help. "Well, I can't wait for an encore."

We held hands like teenagers throughout the entire movie.

"That was really good," I lied as we made our way back to our vehicles, hand in hand.

"No, it wasn't," he replied, chuckling.

We both laughed as we reached my car, our breath creating plumes in the cold January night air. "You're right. They need to stop with those movies."

Karson gently pushed me up against my car and then boxed me in with his arms. "I really want to throw you on the back of my bike and take you to my place, but I'm not going to. I'm gonna be a gentleman and leave you with this."

He leaned down slowly and nipped my bottom lip with his teeth before pressing his lips to mine. The kiss was searing and toe-curling, and so much better than the one in the theater, if that was possible. I instinctively wrapped my arms around his neck as he pressed his hard body into mine. Soon, his hands found my waist, and he ran them up and down over my hips as our tongues and lips continued their dance. It didn't even bother me that the one in the cast was heavy on my hip.

Kissing him felt so natural, but thrilling. His body molded perfectly against mine, but felt exhilarating at the same time. My fingernails raking through the short hair on the back of his head had him groaning into my mouth, and I could feel how much he wanted me, the evidence pressed into my belly. I reached his ear and stroked my fingers over it and the hoop there.

"Good night, Scottlin," he whispered, sounding pained as he pressed his forehead against mine and pierced me with his stormy gaze.

"Good night, Karson," I whispered, wishing the night didn't have to end.

He pushed off me and opened my car door after I'd disarmed it with a beep. He closed it after I got in, then I watched as he went to his bike and slung his leg over the seat. He pulled his phone from his pocket and began typing awkwardly with one finger.

Was he texting another girl so quickly after our date? I frowned and pushed the button to start the car. Before I could put it in gear and drive off, my phone lit up.

Karson: Text me when you get home so I know you got there okay.

I grinned and went to look at him out the window, but he was already zooming out of the parking lot.

I wished our date could have lasted longer, but I was glad when I got home. I was tired from work and the excitement from earlier. The movie had relaxed me, and Karson's kisses had definitely been a rush.

As I put my purse and keys down, I smiled, thinking about the night we'd had. Aside from the vampires, it had been almost perfect. But even with the incident in the parking lot of Burger Bar, it had been kind of cool to see an elf use his abilities. These types of things fascinated me. All magic did. I just wished I was a full witch so I could do all kinds of cool things, too.

I reached for the pack of matches on top of my fridge and lit a candle. I remembered my mother flicking her wrist to light candles in our home as I was growing up. I didn't have that talent. That being said, I wouldn't trade my natural healing abilities for parlor tricks. Curing ailments and healing people was so much more satisfying and made me feel like I had a purpose in life.

After lighting the vanilla-scented candle, I went into my room, stripped out of my clothes, washed my face, and settled onto my sofa to catch up on whatever I had recorded. My phone chimed with a text.

Len: I miss U

I huffed and ignored the text. Responding to it would only encourage him further, and I couldn't do that to him. I didn't miss Len. The connection just hadn't been there, nor was I interested in exploring another go at our relationship. He didn't make my stomach dance with butterflies, or cause heat to spread to my core like Karson did. I needed passion in my life, not mundane.

I set the phone on the end table and sat on the sofa. After picking up the remote, I found what I needed to continue my binge-watching of the newest series I'd become obsessed with, when I heard my phone chime with another text.

If that was Len, I was gonna snap . . .

Karson: You make it home okay?

Oh no! I was supposed to text him.

Me: Yes. Sorry

Karson: I'll punish you later for making me wait. Sleep well, beautiful

I smiled.

Me: I will. You too. xxoo

God, we were already being sappy. And we hadn't even slept together yet.

CHAPTER 18

KARSON

*S*itting in the back of the courtroom, I could do nothing but observe. Memories of five years ago, when Uncle Will had been sentenced for assault, flooded me. He hadn't liked the punishment doled out to him, and had used his affliction to sting a Court member. Unfortunately for everyone involved, the man had fallen and hit his head, almost dying. Thank the gods he'd survived.

But I wasn't here today for my uncle. I was here to see if his son was going to suffer the same punishment as his father. After dressing in jeans, a hoodie reading *Welcome to the Jungle*, and my black boots, I'd taken my bike to the courthouse so I could hear Jalen's fate.

There were very few people in the galley of the windowless courtroom. Addie Beaumont cleared her throat and began speaking. "Jalen Andrew Kane, please stand."

We stood as ordered, and once the Court members took their seats, she instructed us all to sit, which we did.

I looked to the defendant's table to see Jalen stand up, a bit of white-blond stubble covering his jawline.

Mathilde Augustine, a witch on the Court, began, "The charge is breach of confidentiality among the supernatural; specifically, circumventing the systems put in place to protect the town by means of electronic hacking. The defendant has pled guilty."

Jalen nodded.

Mayor Barbie Stuart, a busty blond woman in her forties, pierced my cousin with an icy stare. "Well, Mr. Kane, what do you have to say for yourself before you face sentencing?"

As Jalen seemed to be grasping for words, I felt an overwhelming need to speak up. When my cousin stammered and seemed frustrated, I could hold back no longer. I stood up in the galley of the courtroom and, remembering how I was scolded before for interrupting, I raised my hand. "May I speak on behalf of the, uh, defendant?"

The mayor narrowed her eyes at me, then glared at my cousin. "Is this what you want?"

Jalen nodded. "Yes."

Mayor Stuart, still with an impassive face, nodded slightly. "Very well. Karson Kane, you may speak."

I stood and went to stand near Jalen.

"Mr. Kane, how long have you known the defendant?" Mathilde asked.

"My whole life," I replied, smiling slightly at my cousin.

"You got your memories back!" Jalen blurted.

I nodded and grinned, but the entire Court narrowed their eyes at him.

"Do not speak unless you're spoken to!" Mathilde snapped.

Jalen shrunk down in his seat a little bit and mouthed, "Sorry."

She turned her attention back to me. "I see," she continued. "And has he always been sneaky and deceitful?"

I shook my head. "Not in the least. In fact, not ever. Jalen's a good dude."

"Do you trust him to keep your innermost secrets?" she asked, a smirk playing on her wrinkled lips.

I nodded slowly, then looked at Jalen. "I trust him with my very life. He risked everything to get me to come back to Havenwood Falls, and I will be forever indebted to him. Please . . ." I stared hard at Mathilde and Mayor Stuart, hoping I could get through to them. "It took almost three days to get my memories back, but thank f— the gods that they did. I needed to be back here. I needed to see my family

89

again. There was no other way for him to get me to come home but to break the rules." I looked at my cousin once again. Then I noticed a redheaded breath of fresh air enter the courtroom and take a seat near the back.

I grinned subtly at Scottlin, but continued. "I was lost, completely lost, until I received that email. When I was angry and grieving, I left this town. I let my emotions cloud my judgement." I stopped to heave in a big breath and then blow it out. "But it wasn't the right decision. I've been wandering aimlessly for two years—until I received that email." I looked over at the Court members seated at the dais. "Yes, he hacked your system. Broke your laws . . . these rules." Then I looked at Mathilde Augustine. "But he didn't hurt you, or this town. Nobody found out about us. We're all okay. Right? His dad's in prison. His mom is dead. You blame him for wanting some family around when he was stressed about Uncle Will getting released soon?"

Mathilde's brow furrowed. "William Kane has a bit still left to serve. Why would you think he was getting out so soon? He almost killed a Court member. We don't take kindly to that."

"But he didn't kill him. He used his affliction because he was angry. He didn't want to kill him," Jalen blurted out. "My dad looked devastated that day, I could tell. He'd just wanted to sting him a little. Not kill him."

The memories of what happened to Mihail Petran, a moroi vampire, came flooding back to me. I noticed the Petran seat was empty today. Because of the history? I set my jaw and looked at Mathilde. "He's right. Uncle Will was devastated."

Barbie Stuart pounded her gavel and glared at me. "No speaking out of turn!"

I clamped my mouth shut and nodded slightly in acknowledgment.

Jalen whispered something to me, and I said, "We were under the assumption that Uncle William was getting released soon. Is that not the case?"

Mathilde replied, "He has served his five years, but he got into some trouble while on the inside, so his time in supernatural prison has been extended a bit. He also will still need to serve six weeks in the sheriff's jail."

Jalen looked as frustrated and angry as I felt. "How much longer?"

Mathilde looked down at a paper in her hand through her glasses. "An extra month."

I breathed a sigh of relief. So did Jalen.

"We need an hour recess to make a decision on your punishment, young man. Reconvene at thirteen hundred hours. Court is dismissed." Mayor Stuart pounded her gavel.

I gave my cousin a hug.

"Thanks for doing that for me."

Nodding, I clapped him on the shoulder. "It was the least I could do. I just hope it helps."

"Well, I appreciate it."

"I'm going to grab food. Can I bring you something?"

He nodded. "Yes, please."

"I'm going to get sandwiches. Any requests?" I asked.

He shook his head. "Nope, I'll take anything."

I made my way to Scottlin and smiled down at her. "Thanks for being here."

She leaned up on tiptoe and pecked me on the lips. "It's my lunch break. I've been taking long ones lately, so why stop now?"

Chuckling, I grabbed her hand and led her out of the courtroom. "I'm headed out to get lunch for Jalen and me. You're joining me."

She laughed. "Of course I am."

We left the courthouse hand in hand and walked to Daily Knead.

CHAPTER 19

KARSON

I shouldn't have eaten the whole sandwich. Now, as I sat in the courtroom waiting for the stony-faced Court to dole out its punishment, my stomach was in knots and so not agreeing with being full.

Scottlin seemed to sense my unease, and she squeezed my hand while seated next to me.

"Will the defendant please rise," Addie said.

Mayor Stuart removed her reading glasses and pierced Jalen with her light gray stare. "You knew what you did was blatantly wrong. Permission to contact your cousin and bring him back home would have been granted if you'd only asked, and we could have taken proper measures. Instead, you chose to rebel and break our rules, potentially putting our town's people at risk. That said, in light of your cousin's testimony, combined with the fact that we are already housing one Kane in prison, I hereby sentence you to three days of jail, which have already been completed, a one-thousand-dollar fine, and one hundred hours of community service, to be completed within six months."

Jalen nodded, looking relieved.

"One more thing, and listen to me good. If you ever use your hacking skills to break the wards again, it'll be supernatural prison for you. And you don't want that. Trust me. Are we clear?"

Jalen swallowed hard and nodded. "Yes, ma'am. Won't happen again."

She pounded her gavel. "Court is adjourned."

Addie approached him. "The wards were a bitch to put right again. Don't do that shit again."

He smiled sheepishly. "I won't. Sorry. Can I get my stuff now?"

She nodded. "Of course. Follow me."

"Meet you out front," I said to him as I led Scottlin toward the door that would take us to the stairwell leading up and out of the secret part of City Hall.

Jalen looked drained as I dropped him off at home. I knew he was anxious to charge his phone and sleep in his own bed. I, however, did not want to sit around at home, and decided I should probably go find myself a job. I grabbed my keys and took a short ride through town.

With my bike idling outside of Tragic Ink, I took some deep breaths and pulled my phone from my pocket. I hit the contact icon for the tattoo shop in Colorado Springs and waited while it rang.

Dex answered.

"Hey, it's Karson."

"Hey, dude. When you coming back? Keep getting people in here looking for you."

"About that." I raked my fingers through my hair. "Is G there?"

"Nah, he's gone for a few days, man."

"Can you tell him I won't be coming back?"

Dex gasped. "What? Why?"

I decided to make a long story short. "I moved back home."

"Where's that? I thought you said you didn't know when I asked you last time."

"I, uh, suddenly remembered. Take care, man."

I ended the call, not wanting to talk about it any longer. We only worked in cash there, so it wasn't like I had a final paycheck to look forward to. Thank the gods for the small stash of cash I'd found at home to get me by. I had a few things in the apartment, but I'd take a day trip to Springs to get that stuff later.

Now, with both hands on the handlebars, I stared up at the second story over Howe's Herbal Shoppe, where Tragic Ink was, and saw the lights on.

"Here goes nothing," I whispered to myself, not knowing what to expect, since Scottlin told me Rowdy had closed HF Ink and this was now the only shop in town.

After passing the smelly herbal store, I rounded the corner and climbed the stairs. The door chimed above my head as I entered. The smell of incense and the sound of heavy metal music playing made me smile.

I was surprised to see Gwen Facharro, a friend from high school I had art class and a lot of detention with, sitting in a chair, tattooing something onto the upper arm of a human with a shaved head and lots of muscles.

"I'll be right with you," she said without looking up.

"It's fine. I'm not in a rush." I smirked.

The needle immediately halted, and Gwen looked up. Her eyes went big, and her mouth dropped open.

"Excuse me," she barely spit out to the customer before setting the gun on the tray next to her, yanking off her gloves, and rushing over to me.

She squealed as I picked her up and gave her tiny ass a hug. "Karson!"

"I'm back, baby," I said, staring into her pretty green eyes. "I love the hair, by the way," I added.

She raked her fingers through her hair, as short and as pale as mine. "Thanks."

"You work here now?"

She nodded. "Own it, actually. Opened it a couple years ago."

"I was gonna go see Rowdy, but I heard HF Ink is closed."

She nodded. "Yeah, Rowdy died."

My eyes widened. "He died?"

"Yes," she replied, frowning. "Sucks."

Deciding I'd get details later, I said, "Look, I won't beat around the bush. I need a job."

"Thank fuck," the human blurted, and we both looked over at him. He was smiling at us and said, "It took me, like, six weeks to get this appointment because she's the main game in town."

"Oh, shut it, Hank," she said. "You know I hate people."

Hank and I both laughed.

"What do you say?" I asked, hopeful.

"Of course you're hired. If Rowdy trusted you, so do I. Plus, I've seen your work on folks around town. It's good stuff." She sighed. "Besides, Hank's right. I've been swamped, plus with all the traveling I've been doing . . . but you know I don't have the patience to be peopling, anyway. But, with you here, it'll be nice to have an extra set of hands."

"Sweet!" I said, my stomach stirring with excitement. "That was easy."

She punched me lightly in the arm. "You knew I'd hire you. But, uh . . ." She pointed at the cast on my hand.

I smiled, embarrassed. "Yeah, Karson's temper for the win."

She snorted and made her way back to Hank. After sitting, she grabbed a fresh set of rubber gloves from a box and put them on. "Right. You angry asshole."

"I'm better now, I swear. And the hand . . . cast comes off in two weeks. It's my strong hand, though. Unfortunately."

She glanced at me briefly, then picked up the gun. "Got some new ink, I see."

"Yeah, I worked at a shop in Springs. I see you don't have any more room for any new ink." I jutted my chin at her sleeved-up arms and shoulders. As she was in a black tank top, I could see most of them. They were badass, and she had done them all herself. Well, except her registry tat, of course.

She grinned. "So what brought you back to town?" She put the needle to Hank's skin to continue the shading she was doing on his upper arm.

I launched into the entire story, leaving out the memory issues for the sake of the human in the room. She glanced at me a couple of times when parts of the story didn't quite make sense, but I knew she understood.

After sitting and visiting with her for about half an hour, and watching her amazing work on Hank, I left the shop, happy things seemed to be working out for me.

Bored, I drove my bike to the Havenwood Falls Medical Center to see Scottlin. As I entered the ER, I stopped short when I saw her standing behind the counter of the nurse's station, talking to the same guy I had seen her eating with at the pizza joint. This time, though, the man wore an EMT uniform and was leaning over the counter, reaching up to finger one of her braids. She smiled at him and laughed at something he'd said while moving back and out of his reach. When he put his hand on top of hers on the counter and she frowned at it, the rage I was suppressing came bubbling up.

I stalked toward the counter and smacked my good hand down on it. This caused not only Scottlin and the guy to look up, but everyone around to startle.

"Karson," Scottlin said, smiling tightly at me. "I didn't expect to see you here . . ."

"Who's this? A *friend*?" I asked her, but was looking into the guy's brown eyes.

He stood up straight and was just a couple inches shorter than me. He lifted his chin and said, "Who the hell are you?"

"Karson, let's go into my office, okay?" Scottlin said, coming around the desk and grabbing me by the arm.

"Nah, I'm good," I said, feeling the magic inside of me begin to stir. I wanted to sting on this guy so bad, it hurt. For no other reason than he was looking at Scottlin in a way that only I should be looking at her.

The EMT put his hand on his hip and looked past me at Scottlin. He pointed at me. "Who is this asshole?"

That was it. Without thinking, I reared my left arm back and smashed my fist into his cheek.

The guy swore in pain and then took a swing at me.

I stepped back before he could make contact, then turned on my heel and stormed out of the hospital. "Fuck!"

Scottlin didn't even yell out my name or try to stop me.

As soon as I located my bike, I hopped on and rode off with no destination at all.

CHAPTER 20

KARSON

"*D*ude, you need anger management or something," Jalen said, the video game controller in his hand, the game paused on the screen after I told him everything.

I plopped down next to him. "No shit."

"You said she told you that guy was just a friend or something, didn't she?" He stared at me.

I looked back at him and was happy to see he looked rested, the dark circles that had been under his eyes gone, and he'd shaved and gotten a haircut. "Yeah, I guess."

"You're the one who's gonna be in court next. That dude could charge you with assault. And you'll be in even bigger trouble with the Court since he's human. You could have really hurt him."

I snorted. "I probably did."

"Let me know if you need bail money," he joked with a sardonic laugh. He threw me the extra controller and changed the game so we could both play.

I welcomed the distraction, and we ended up playing for a good three hours, during which time I didn't check my phone once. We had a nice catch-up about how I'd gone to see my dad, how he'd given me the bike, and how Gwen had hired me at the shop.

I got up to get something to eat and plucked my phone out of my pocket to see I had no texts or calls.

Great.

I sighed in disappointment that Scottlin hadn't responded to the apology text I'd sent after leaving the hospital.

After pocketing the phone, I found a couple frozen dinners and heated up the oven to get them going for us. I obviously wasn't going anywhere tonight, even though I should be apologizing to Scottlin in person. She was already off work, and I contemplated going to her apartment and begging for her forgiveness.

I ran the idea by my cousin. He shook his head. "Nope, nope, nope. Chicks need time to cool off. She'll probably slam the door in your face, bro."

"Because you're such an expert on women? You're twenty-six and still single."

"First off, asswipe, you asked me. Second, I'm single for a reason." He used the controller to kill three zombies heading toward his avatar.

I snorted. "And why's that?"

"Because women are too much work. Especially the elven chicks. God, they're moody."

I sat back on the couch and folded my arms across my chest. "Where are there female elves in this town? Our moms were the only ones."

Jalen cleared his throat. "I have to leave Havenwood Falls to find them, but they're out there."

"So date a human. Or a witch or something."

"Fuck those witches. And humans . . . too much work to hide what we are."

I shook my head. "I disagree. There's nothing to hide. Our ears are glamoured from them around here, and aside from the quick healing and affliction, we're just like them."

"And all the delicious flowers," he said, laughing. Then he went back into the zone, chopping off the head of a zombie who was ambling toward his character. The oven beeped, and I got up to put the dinners in. I shook my head at the cracked door that I had caused and vowed to research tomorrow how to replace the glass. I'd YouTube it if I had to.

After I set the timer, I checked my phone. No texts.

I began to pace the living room where Jalen continued to furiously press the buttons on the controller. I was too distracted to play, though. I checked the time on my watch and saw that it was nearing seven p.m.

"Fuck it," I said, heading toward the front door. I snatched my coat off the rack and called out to Jalen, "Don't let the TV dinners burn. They'll be done in about fifteen."

He laughed and said, "She's gonna slam the door in your face, and I'm going to eat both dinners. Byeeee."

I flipped him off. After closing and locking the door behind me, I fast-walked to my bike, hopped on, started it up, and headed toward Scottlin's apartment to try to do the right thing.

"Go away, Karson," Scottlin said weakly, muffled behind the door.

I put my forehead against the door and said, "Please just let me in? I want to explain. Please."

No response greeted me.

"Scottlin, I'm sorry. I have a temper. I just want to talk to you. I didn't mean to do that. You've just . . . dammit." I raked my fingers through my hair. "I just lost it when I saw that guy with you. I want you all to myself. I'm selfish, but I promise I'm not a jealous asshole. It's just that I've got all these fucking feelings for you and obviously need to learn how to express them better." I sighed, then knocked. "Can't we just talk? Please? I miss your pretty smile and beautiful laugh. I need to know you don't hate me."

I heard no movement from behind the door. There was just nothing. I waited and knocked for five more minutes, but the door never opened. I looked down when I saw a small slip of paper slide out from under the door. I picked it up to see Dr. Espensen's card.

Okay, I can take a hint.

Defeated, I slowly made my way down the stairs and out to the parking lot, tossing the business card into a nearby trash can. After starting up my bike, I looked up at the window to Scottlin's apartment and saw her face staring down at me for just a split second before she flicked the curtain back into place. With a heavy sigh, I lifted my facemask with the skull on it over my mouth and nose to protect from the cold. I should probably wear a helmet, but I didn't give a shit as I steered my way out of the icy parking lot.

As I rode, I internally kicked myself for fucking things up with Scottlin. We'd barely gotten started, but I knew she was into me. Until my temper reared its ugly head. It had been ruining things for me since I was a teen, and I needed to get a handle on it. I knew my life would never change for the better until I dealt with all the shit with my mom, and the two years of my life I lost because of it.

But how?

I was never one for counseling or therapy, even though I knew I should probably talk to someone. I just wasn't sure where to start. I wasn't sure I would even go through with it, and of course I'd just impulsively thrown away that business card.

Then Scottlin's pretty face materialized in my mind. Her beautiful blue eyes. Her pretty smile. Her soft-spoken and caring mannerisms. Her silky hair. Her beautiful mind. Maybe if I got some help for my temper, she would give me a second chance. Maybe I could prove to her that I wasn't an impulsive asshole.

I reached my house quickly enough and found Jalen right where I'd left him—and true to his word, he'd eaten both dinners.

Without turning around, he said, "She slammed the door in your face, didn't she?"

I threw my jacket and mask onto the dining room table, then plopped down next to him. "No, she never even opened the door."

"You shoulda listened to me, man." He chuckled.

I picked up the extra controller. "I need to kill something."

He grunted and switched the game back to zombies.

"So where is Uncle Will imprisoned at, anyway?" I asked, wondering why he hadn't suggested visiting him.

"Supernatural prison."

I resisted the urge to roll my eyes. "No shit? Where's that?"

He lifted a shoulder as his character dodged a zombie and then did a roundhouse kick to its head. "Through some portal near the falls. They took him off in cuffs, and I haven't seen him in five years."

I shuddered as my avatar used its machete to chop off a zombie's head. "I wonder what kind of prison it is?"

"I tried asking around, but I only got vague answers. Some island the fae run in another part of the world. I'm not sure. I asked if I could visit, and they laughed at me."

I hit pause on the game and looked at my cousin.

He stared at me expectantly.

"Tell me this. What's the real reason you wanted me back here? Do you really need help with Uncle Will once he gets out, or what?"

Jalen let out a sigh and set his controller down. "I don't know, man. I missed you. Gavin only comes here a couple days a month, my mom's fuckin' gone, and I miss my dad. I just don't know what to expect when he gets back. Plus, you had been gone way too long. After you took off, I thought, 'Oh, he'll come back before the lunar cycle. He's not that stupid.' But you *were* that stupid. Thank the gods you never changed your email address or I would have never fuckin' found you. Your cell number was disconnected almost immediately."

"You waited two years to get in touch with me, though . . . kinda weird."

He nodded. "Yeah. I was going to earlier, but Gavin said to give you time."

I thought about what he said, and Gavin had been right. A month or six after I left would not have been enough time for me to have learned my lesson. I would still have been that angry guy who didn't know how to grieve the abusive mother who didn't deserve to be grieved.

I thought about today and how I'd messed things up with Scottlin because of my temper. *I guess I still am that angry guy . . .*

"You did the right thing," I assured him. "Now . . . I need to do the right thing."

I went over to the laptop and booted it up as I walked with it back to the sofa. "I need to talk to someone."

"What, like a shrink?" he asked, surprised.

"Your mom died in an accident, and that sucks. But she didn't do horrible things to you. I gotta get a grip on my shit." I typed "grief counselors" into the search bar.

Jalen threw the controller down and turned all the way to face me. "What in the hell are you talking about?"

Looking up from the computer, I took a deep breath and looked into my cousin's eyes. He'd been my best friend my whole life, and should have known these things, but never did because I never said shit about it when we were kids.

"You sure you wanna know, man? Because once I tell you, you can't unhear this shit."

"Fucking spill it. Now."

"Okay . . ." With more bravery than I felt, I word-vomited everything that happened to me for as long as I could remember— which started about age four. The cigarette burns. Being locked in closets and rooms for hours and sometimes days. The verbal abuse. Her forcing vodka down my throat just to get me to stop crying and go to sleep. The way she told me she hated me so many times when she was drunk, or high, or both. I went on for half an hour, barely taking a breath in between stories. Once I was done, my eyes blurred with unshed tears from letting it all out . . . but it had felt good. So good.

My cousin's eyes were glistening, and he turned away and sucked in a deep breath. "What the fuck, man? Where was your dad?"

"Working," I replied bitterly. "Always fucking working. He knew she was an addict, but didn't know about all the things she did to me —just some. And I haven't even told him half the shit I just told you, but he knew enough right before I left Havenwood Falls after finding her dead. I'm sure that's why he never came looking for me. He just knew."

"Well, that sucks, and now I'm pissed off." He leaned forward and rested his forearms on his basketball shorts.

I clapped him on the back. "It's okay. What sucks is . . . when I lived in Springs, I didn't have to deal with this bullshit because I forgot all about it."

"Well, that's one positive to you having been gone, I guess," he murmured. "Now I feel kinda bad bringing you back."

"Well, don't. Because the problem is, I always had pain in my chest . . . in my soul. I always knew something was terribly wrong, but I could never pinpoint what it was, because I couldn't remember. I couldn't go see a doctor, because what would I tell him? I couldn't go see a shrink, because they'd just want to know about my past and why I was so wound up and in pain. So the not remembering kinda backfired now. It sucks to relive all this shit, but it's kinda freeing to talk about it, too."

Jalen stared at the ground, his hands folded together over his legs. "I guess I can understand that."

I looked down at the laptop and clicked on a few sites, saving them to call later to see if there was someone in this town I could talk to.

CHAPTER 21

SCOTTLIN

J sat on my bed with my fingers in my ears and the volume on the TV in my bedroom up loud. I couldn't take listening to Karson's pleas that were breaking my heart, or the pounding on my door. I just hoped he'd leave soon, before one of my neighbors called the cops on him. He definitely didn't need any legal trouble, and it seemed the entire Kane family attracted that stuff like flies on honey. I was glad slipping him the business card had the desired effect and got him to leave. Hopefully he was off to get some real help.

I'd had to beg Len to not call the sheriff on Karson. He had wanted to press charges, but I convinced him not to. I told him he was a patient who'd developed a little crush on me, but didn't elaborate further. I was a coward for not telling him how deeply I'd fallen for the guy, and how I had been thinking about a future with him in it after just one date. No, I couldn't hurt Len like that. We had agreed to be friends, but the man still looked at me the same way he always had—with longing and admiration. I couldn't take it.

I'd had to put my professional mask into place as I had treated his very bruised but thankfully not broken cheekbone. Karson had only opened up a small cut with his knuckles, and I was surprised he could do that much damage with his weak hand. He was lucky he wasn't sporting two casts at this point.

The boy had a temper . . . and I didn't want anything to do with someone like that. I wasn't sure why he was so angry—and at the most peculiar of times, too—but I supposed it wasn't any of my business. He had been fun, but there was no way I was going to waste my time with someone with anger issues. He was way more drama than I was ready to take on.

But hadn't I known he was kind of a loose cannon from the first day I met him? Why had he punched that oven? I just figured he had been frustrated over the fact that his memories hadn't returned. But to punch something that hard over something like that—who does that?

Somebody deeply hurting, that's who.

I squeezed my eyes shut and tried to block out Karson's beautiful face and all the sweet and kind things he'd ever done and said to me. All the pain I'd seen floating behind his stormy gaze that I had ignored and had brushed off as something about his race.

Breathing out a calming breath, I slowly reopened my eyes and stared unseeing at the TV. I had obviously never fallen victim to the memory wards around the town, and I never planned to. If Karson had grown up here, he had to have known that his memory would be gone if he stayed away too long.

So why had he?

I took my fingers out of my ears and was met with only the sound of the TV. I picked up the remote and muted it.

Silence. Deafening silence. Karson had left.

Because I was a masochist, I looked at my phone. No other texts from him. I hadn't responded to his apology earlier because I had been so furious. Since I'd calmed some, I contemplated texting him back. But what would I say? *I forgive you? It's okay?* No, neither of those things applied here. I threw my phone down in frustration and unmuted the TV. I needed to sleep on this.

"Good morning, doc," Shayna said with a grin.

"Good morning," I replied, the large steaming cup from Coffee Haven warming my hand.

I made my way to my office. After hanging up my coat, I went around and sat at my desk. I pushed the button to boot up my computer and opened my daily calendar. A list of appointments greeted me, along with the blocks of hours I would be on call in the ER. One appointment caught my eye, flashing like a beacon: *2:00 p.m. Cast Removal – Karson Kane.*

I heaved a sigh. It had been almost two weeks since Karson had punched Len. He had sent the apology text, then a few days later, another about him missing me. I had ignored that one, too. I hoped that ignoring him would make his beautiful face and eyes fade from my memory.

But they hadn't. Not even remotely. I woke every day thinking about Karson, and thoughts of him would consume me as I lay down at night to go to sleep, with no break in between—even while I was working. It was absolute torture. I kept telling myself that it would fade eventually. That I would get over him and find someone else soon. A nice, normal man, who was not hotheaded or violent. And I believed the words I constantly told myself.

In my head, they made sense. *I could do this.* But in my heart . . . those stirrings just wouldn't let him go. He had embedded himself into my very soul, and the pain in my chest wasn't going to ease up any time soon. There was something about Karson that was different from the men I had dated before, and I was kicking myself for letting him in so easily and so quickly. No, that list wasn't very long, but I had been in relationships, and none of them had felt as fiery or passionate as this one had.

What was wrong with me? Two kisses and a couple of dates, and here I was practically panting over a guy I barely knew. I certainly hadn't gone all the way with him, but goddess . . . I so wanted to.

Snap out of it, Scottlin! I screamed at myself. *Yes, let's get out of la-la land and live in reality. Bad boys are no good for you. Find yourself a man who is stable and sweet.*

The phone in my pocket vibrated. I pulled it up and looked at the screen:

HFMC-ER: You're needed in the ER STAT

Without more time to dwell on Karson, I raced out of my office, slammed the door shut behind me, and went into the ER to face the latest emergency.

I stopped short when I arrived to see a woman lying on a gurney with her throat looking like raw hamburger. A nurse ran around me and placed a cloth against the woman's neck, then climbed on top of the gurney to hold it there while the EMTs pushed her into a room.

I spotted Len as one of those EMTs, but paid him no mind. The bruise on his cheek was nothing more than a fading yellow annoyance, and it seemed he was also in the zone, just trying to help the young woman.

"What's your name?" I asked the girl as I ran alongside the gurney.

"Lily," she whispered. "He was so strong. Help me. I'm scared."

I lifted the cloth on her neck and could see her throat had been ripped open. The bleeding had stopped at her carotid, but the exposed skin and muscle showed telltale signs of a wolf's bite.

"Take her to room four. I'll tend to her," I demanded angrily.

"What can I do?" Len asked, looking at me with fearful eyes.

I shook my head. "Nothing. I got it from here."

The nurse who had hopped on the gurney jumped down, and I looked at her. "Can you give the patient sixty milligrams of Toradol IM, times one dose now and one gram of Rocephin IM, times one dose now?"

"On it," the nurse said, scurrying out of the room to get the meds.

I looked down at Lily, who was definitely human and didn't look a day over twenty-one. I smiled at her. "It's going to be okay. Can you tell me what happened?"

Her eyes fluttered shut as if she was going to lose consciousness. "He was so strong."

She'd already said that. I tried a different approach. "Where were you today, Lily?"

Her eyelashes flickered and then opened, coffee-colored irises meeting me. "The falls. He was so cute . . . so beautiful. I thought he was into me . . . then he turned into a monster . . . Oh, God . . ."

She began to sob, then eventually fell into unconsciousness, and I knew I had to report this to the Court. But first, some pictures. I pulled my phone from my pocket and opened the camera app. After I snapped half a dozen pictures of her injuries, the nurse came in and administered the medication I'd ordered.

"Anything else I can do?" she asked.

"Yeah, try to find out her last name and address. I'll stay with her to make sure she's stable."

"I think she had a purse. On it." The nurse left the room.

When I was sure the door was shut tightly, I placed my hands over Lily's cheeks and closed my eyes. My hands began to grow warm with magic, and as I felt it swirling inside me, I let it rush out of my fingertips. A faint yellow glow only someone supernatural could see began to light up her face.

I leaned down and whispered into her right ear. "You were attacked by an animal out by the falls. You shouldn't go out there alone. There was no boy. You were by yourself."

Still unconscious, Lily heaved in a big breath, and then let it out again.

I removed my hands and sighed. After carefully removing the makeshift dressing, I tossed the bloodied thing in the trash and then cleaned the wound carefully. It had healed a lot, but not completely— which was my objective. She couldn't walk out of here with no wounds. And she most certainly couldn't go around telling people a man turned into a wolf. I was pretty sure I had removed any werewolf venom she may have had in her system, as I knew some wolves could create other ones like we read about in folklore, and in this case, I didn't know what wolf had done this. Better safe than sorry, I say.

I covered her up with a blanket from the warmer and left the room. I instructed the nurse to start a transfusion, then get her into a room in the ICU, which I knew she probably didn't need, but it would make sense medically to do so.

All was quiet in the ER, but I was drained. I went back to my office, shot off a quick email to the Court that I needed to speak to them, hung up my lab coat, and grabbed my purse. *Coffee Haven, here I come.*

CHAPTER 22

KARSON

*M*y calendar app chimed on my phone. I pulled it off the nightstand and looked at it: *2 p.m. cast removal.* Freaking finally.

But how awkward was that going to be? I would have to see Scottlin, and she would probably make someone else do it. I wanted to see her badly . . . but I couldn't take that look of rejection and disappointment on her face.

I flung back the covers, took care of business, brushed my teeth, and went downstairs to see it was all quiet. *Jalen must still be in bed.* I wandered into the garage. After flipping on the light, I was relieved to see that Dad's tools were still sitting on his giant workbench.

I looked down at my cast, then wandered to the group of saws. "Electric or hand saw?"

Then I saw a new toy Dad must have gotten recently. A Dremmel electric hand saw with a three-inch blade. After putting on a thick work glove, I picked up the tool. It was lightweight, and I could use it with one hand. I flicked the button, and the thing whirred to life.

"You're not doing what I think you're doing, are you?"

I turned to look at Jalen.

"No, but you are," I said with a wicked gleam in my eye, holding up the saw and clicking it off.

Jalen chuckled and walked toward me. "Uncle Ellis bought that when I was replacing some baseboards last year. It's a cool little tool, and I know it can cut through plaster. But are you sure it's safe to take that off? What if your hand is still fucked up?"

"I have an appointment today to get it taken off, but I don't want to see her, so I would rather just avoid some awkward shit if I can."

He nodded. "I hear you."

Before I lost my nerve, I handed the gloves to my cousin and laid my arm down on the workbench. I felt a little better knowing Jalen had already used the tool and knew how to handle it.

"What, now?" he asked, looking at me.

"Yes, now, before I chicken out," I said, taking a deep breath.

He lifted a shoulder and let it fall. "Okay, dude."

I watched him put on the gloves and a pair of safety goggles. He clicked the button.

"Ready?" he asked.

"Yep."

With one hand, Jalen held my arm flat on the bench, and with the other, he slowly began to saw through my cast, starting at the end, near my forearm. It didn't take long for me to feel heat from the saw, and I prayed it wouldn't touch my skin.

I looked down to see that he had successfully cut all the way through to the bottom of the plaster. Occasionally, he would set it down to try to pry the cast apart with his hands. Once he reached my hand, though, the plaster was thicker, and he had to use the tool again.

"Hold very still," he said quietly, tilting his head.

"Just do it, man," I said, wanting the thing off.

He nodded and began to run the saw over my wrist and toward the junction between my thumb and forefinger. He was almost there when we heard, "What the fuck are you clowns doing?"

We both startled, and the saw bit into my bare skin.

"Fuck!" I yelled, pulling my hand away. Blood began to seep out of the plaster as my dad ran toward me.

"Are you guys stupid? What did you think was gonna happen,

trying to get this thing off yourself?" Dad said, handing a paper towel to me.

"I almost had it," Jalen snapped, turning off the saw and jerking his gloves and glasses off. He threw them down on the bench. "You scared us!"

Dad used all his strength to pull the cast the rest of the way off. It shimmied off like a really tight glove. He tossed it onto the bench and looked at the cut, which was bleeding pretty badly. "That's gonna need stitches. Put some clothes on. I'm taking you to the hospital."

I groaned and kept the paper towel wrapped around my hand as I went inside to try to change.

"You and I are gonna have a talk later," I heard Dad say to Jalen.

"What were you doing there, anyway, Dad?" I asked as we pulled up to the front of Havenwood Falls Medical Center. I was trying to do anything to distract myself from thinking about the look Scottlin was gonna give me when she was forced to, yet again, fix my stupidity.

"Ironically," he said, shutting off the ignition and piercing me with his purple eyes, "I was coming over to get that saw. Regina wants crown molding in the dining room, and it's the perfect size."

"Sorry," I said sheepishly.

He just grinned. "The saw still works, I'm sure. But you completely defeated the purpose of removing the cast by winding up here anyway." He pointed to the hospital.

"Let's get this over with," I griped, getting out of the car and cradling my hand while trying to close the car door with my hip.

We walked inside, and thankfully, the ER was empty, save for a couple of staff. I went up to the desk and told Shayna, "I need to see a doctor."

She smiled at me. "Hey, Karson. You're a couple hours early for your appointment, though."

My dad chuckled, and I wanted to elbow him in the ribs. I ignored him instead, and said, "Yeah, about that . . ." I held up my blood-soaked hand.

"Eek!" she said, then picked up the phone and hit some buttons. "Scottlin, you're needed in the ER."

Great . . .

"Imma grab a coffee from the machine. Want one?"

I looked at Dad. "Yeah, and something to eat before I pass out."

He nodded and went toward the machines. While Shayna walked away from the desk, I noticed a vase of roses on it. I took a quick look around, pulled one out of the vase, popped the flower off the stem, and shoved it into my mouth.

Mmmm.

Just then, Scottlin came out in her green scrubs and white medical coat. She looked absolutely stunning, even if she did sport the braids that I wished she'd take down. She was looking down at an electronic tablet in her hand. "What do we have today—" We locked eyes, and after her initial surprise, hers just looked . . . pained. "Mr. Kane, you're early today."

I cringed at the formality with which she'd addressed me.

I was still chewing the rose, and she looked at me funny. "What's in your mouth?"

I shook my head, and swallowed hard. "Nothing."

"Okay . . . well, what are you doing here?"

"First off, please don't call me that. Secondly, I don't need the cast off"—I shoved my hand up toward her—"but I think I need some stitches."

Her features immediately softened. "Oh, Karson, what did you do?" She sighed. "Follow me." I obeyed, subtly sniffing the strawberry scent she left in her wake as she led me into a small room. "Sit."

I sat on the medical table with my feet dangling over the edge while Scottlin closed the door. I swallowed hard. We hadn't been alone in a room together in a while.

"Let me see," she quietly commanded. I held my hand out. She slowly unwrapped the bloody paper towel and set it on the metal table full of tools that stood next to her. She examined the cut, which had stopped bleeding, but was gaping open, and said, "How did this happen?"

I pierced her with a look that said *Do I have to?*

She bit back a smile. "You removed the cast with a saw, didn't you?"

I shook my head. "Nope. Jalen did."

"You couldn't wait a few hours for your appointment?" she asked, turning away to rifle through some drawers.

With her back to me, I decided I had nothing to lose by being honest. "I didn't want to see you."

She froze mid-rifle and paused before saying, "That's understandable." She found what she had been looking for and turned back around. "And how did that work out for you?"

Ouch.

I lifted my chin. "Obviously, not well. So let's get this over with, or else I'll end up begging you to give me a second chance. Again. Which clearly *won't* work out for me."

CHAPTER 23

SCOTTLIN

J kept my face impassive and pretended that his words hadn't cut me deep. Just seeing the sexy man again was painful. I thought I was over him, had moved past all of this, but just hearing his voice and seeing him hurt had me right back at square one. All I wanted to do was fix his wounds, then take him home to give him some more TLC.

In the bedroom.

But I knew that was not best for me. So in response, I said, "I'm saying this as a professional, and not as an ex . . . whatever." I set the suture kit on the tray and looked straight into those stormy purple eyes of his. "You need to learn to control your impulses. Hitting things, punching people, removing casts with very dangerous tools." I looked at all the tattoos on his arms, which were hot, but I had to wonder if those had been impulsive, too. "It's not good for you. Make better decisions, Karson, then maybe we can talk about . . . us."

He looked wounded for a minute, so I decided I wasn't going to use sutures. I was going to heal him so I could send him on his way. The longer I spent alone in this room with this heat crackling between us, the more my resolve would waver. I might agree to give him another chance, and nothing would change with him.

"Thank you," he said quietly.

"How is your hand feeling without the cast?" I asked, trying to ease him into what I was about to do without freaking him out. Sure, he was a supe, but he probably hadn't dealt with being healed supernaturally before.

"Hard to say, feels weak, but I haven't had my coffee yet." He grinned faintly at me.

Just then, someone knocked on the door.

"Come in," I called out.

"Can I just give him this?" a large man carrying a cup of coffee and a muffin asked.

"This is my dad, Ellis," I said. "Dad, this is Scottlin."

"Nice to meet you," I said, rubbing my hands together on my lap.

"Can he eat this in here?" his father asked.

"I don't know. He's pretty accident-prone," I replied, swallowing down a smile.

Dad chuckled. "No, he's not. He's just a hothead."

Even his dad sees it. I just smiled.

"I'll set it down here, and you can have it when you're done with that." He set the coffee and muffin on the counter and poked his head around my shoulders. "Ew," he said before walking out and closing the door behind him.

I chuckled and then pierced Karson with a serious stare. I placed both hands over his injured one. "Stay still, okay?"

He nodded, not breaking eye contact.

My eyes slid closed, and I brought the warmth from my very center up through my chest and into my hands. I didn't need to open my eyes to know they were glowing yellow. Karson's gasp was enough. When I felt the warmth start to fade, I opened my eyes and looked down at the cut.

Completely gone.

I glanced up at him, and his eyes were wide. "So cool!"

I pressed a finger to my lips. "Shhh."

"Why didn't you do that when I broke my hand?" He cleared his throat. "I mean, seems like it would have been easier."

I got up because his beautiful lips and stormy eyes were starting to break my resolve, and I felt like I couldn't breathe. I turned my back to him and threw his bloody paper towels in the trash. "Because you thought I was human. And . . ."

"And what?" he asked eagerly.

I slowly turned around. "I thought maybe wearing that cast could serve as a reminder to, you know, cool your jets, like my grandpa used to say." I smiled weakly. "Plus, there was too much magic going on as it was."

He nodded and held up his hand. "I guess. But thanks for using your juju on me this time."

"I won't hesitate to the next time you come in here."

He stood up and gave me a half grin. "Next time?"

I folded my arms over my chest and simply nodded.

Karson cleared his throat. "Okay, anyway. Um, do you know of any, like, counselors here in town?"

I cocked my head to the side. He didn't seem like the type who talked about his feelings with strangers. "Yes, I know a couple." I cleared my throat. "And I do believe I already gave you a card.

"Um, I, uh, don't have that card anymore."

This didn't surprise me. "You looking for a certain type of therapist?"

He nodded. "Yeah, trauma, PTSD, mommy issues, that type of shit."

Mommy issues? "Yeah, Dr. Espensen. I'll get you another card when we're done."

"Thanks."

God, he was being so sweet and calm. And now he was asking for psych help?

We said nothing else, but I could feel the weight of his stare on me as I finished up jotting notes into his chart. He sat there, still looking at me. I wanted to go sit on his lap, lay my head on his chest, and let him wrap his arms around me.

But, of course, I didn't.

"Let's get you an X-ray to make sure that hand has healed properly, then once you're clear, you can go.

He scooted off the table and lifted his hand. "Thanks."

I pointed to the counter. "Don't forget your breakfast."

He grabbed the items, and I led him out and toward my office. He stood just inside the door as I rummaged through my drawer until I found Dr. Espensen's card. I handed it to him. "Talk to her. She's great."

"Appreciate it," he murmured, shoving it into his jeans pocket.

"Hey. Are you okay?" I asked, meaning it.

"Hopefully, I will be one day, once I get my shit straightened out." He turned and walked out of my office. I was going to follow him to show him where to go, but figured he could read the signs.

I sat down and sighed. Maybe I'd misjudged him? He had a sweet and soft side, but I already knew that. Clearly, he was dealing with some deeper issues that I hoped he could get help for. Half of me wanted to know what they were; the other half just didn't. It was his business, and I hoped talking to someone would help him out.

Mommy issues.

Curiosity got the best of me. I turned to my computer, typed in his name, and found his medical history again. I noted his mother's name, Lyn Kane, and looked her up. *Deceased, December 2016. Overdose.*

With a heavy sigh, I stared at my cup of almost-gone coffee and used my desk phone to dial Alex, my closest friend.

"Hello?"

"Girl, I need coffee," I said.

She laughed. "I'm actually studying at Coffee Haven right now, but I'm almost done. I gotta run a few errands after this. You want the usual?"

"Yes, please. And a scone. I don't care what kind."

"You got it."

"Thanks." I hung up the clunky phone, and my cell vibrated in my pocket. I got up before even looking at it, heading toward the ER to deal with the next emergency.

"Ahh," I said, sipping the hot, caffeinated nectar.

"You're addicted," Alex said, sitting on the bench with me outside the hospital. It was chilly, but we were bundled up, and the sun was shining. It glinted off the sparkly snow piled up on the grass surrounding the medical center.

"I know." I sighed.

Alex twisted the clunky ring she always wore on her thumb and stared hard at me with her mocha-colored eyes. "What's wrong? Something's wrong."

I chewed my lip and broke her stare. "Karson came into the ER today."

"Is he okay?" Alex asked.

I laughed, but there wasn't much humor in it. "He had his cousin use a saw to get his cast off."

"Dumb boys," she replied with a snicker.

"Right? Well, he said some things that pulled on my heartstrings a little, ya know. Hinted at a second chance."

She placed her hand on mine, and I stared down at the contrast between her warm caramel-colored skin and my freckly whiteness. "And are you going to give him one?"

I shook my head. "Nah. I can't. He's got things he needs to fix first."

"Don't we all," she replied. "But I'm sure it's hard."

I nodded. "Yeah, it is. He's so cute and sexy, and I'm so attracted to him."

"Sex does not a relationship make, girlfriend," she replied. "But it can be fun for a while."

"I wouldn't know," I replied dryly. "Never had one of those types of relationships. I just seem to attract the boring ones or the damaged ones."

"Who's damaged?" Alex asked, lifting her chai latte to her lips.

"Karson just said he had some issues and needed to talk to someone, so I referred him. He didn't elaborate, and I didn't ask."

"Well, could it be his issues are what's causing his anger?"

Uh oh, the doctorate degree Alex was working on was about to start coming out.

I shrugged. "Not sure."

"Well, they're probably connected." She stood up. "I gotta go, kiddo. Holler at me later if you want to go get a drink or something."

Like I ever went to bars. I could only imagine the kind of guy I would pick up at one.

CHAPTER 24

KARSON

The next day, I found myself looking up at the small house-turned-office with a wooden sign reading *Havenwood Falls Psychology & Counseling* swinging in the wind. I walked up the three rickety steps and blew warm air into my hands before knocking on the front door. It opened quickly, and an older lady dressed sorta hippie-chic opened it up. She smiled warmly at me with kind brown eyes.

"Hi, I'm Julie Espensen. You must be Karson?"

I shook her hand. "Yes."

"You can hang your coat over there. Then have a seat," she instructed, after leading me down a hallway to an office with a large oak partners desk in the corner and a plush blue sofa opposite it. On one wall hung many framed certificates. On her desk were multiple photographs of children and adults.

I hung up my coat and sat down, feeling nervous and just wanting to bolt. I wasn't sure I had made the right decision coming here. But I also knew I couldn't keep going on the way I had been.

"So, Karson, what brings you in?" she asked, pushing a curly gray strand of hair behind her ear as she smiled at me. I noticed she had rings on almost every finger.

I swallowed and licked my lips before saying, "I've, ah, been told I need some anger management therapy or something."

She began scrawling on a notepad in her lap. "I see. And do you think you need anger management?"

I shrugged. "Yeah. I tried running away, and that didn't work. Came back just as angry. My dad says I'm a hothead."

"And do you think you are?"

"I guess."

She jotted some more notes. "Tell me about your childhood."

And there it was. I knew she was going to ask, just like they always did in the movies. Deciding not to fight it, I took a deep breath and began talking about my earliest memories of my mother. I didn't think she got a word in edgewise, as she furiously jotted down notes while I spoke. Then I told her about my leaving Havenwood Falls, and what had gone on since my return, leaving out the memory glitch, since I was pretty sure the doc was human.

I glanced at the clock and could see forty minutes had gone by. *Wow.*

I was proud I hadn't shed a tear, but I had to hold a few back a couple of times. The weirdest thing, though, was that I felt like a huge weight had been lifted off me. Even more so than when I had told Jalen about it.

Dr. Espensen talked to me some more in her mild-mannered way, said some things about guilt, and tried to help me understand that none of what happened to me as a kid was my fault. We set an appointment for me to come back in a week. I paid her cash for the visit and left through the front door with a little bit of a spring in my step.

After arriving home, I glanced at the clock on the microwave to see it was nearing five p.m. It was a Friday night, and I was feeling restless. I plunked my keys and phone onto the dining room table and went to the living room to find Jalen—surprise, surprise—playing video games. Well, he was a video game tester, after all, but didn't he ever get sick of it?

I parked my ass on the opposite side of the couch and looked at the screen. Some kind of robot-looking creatures were chasing humans through the streets of a big city.

"The fuck is this?" I asked, intrigued.

"Brand new," he said as his avatar ran into a nearby building and began climbing the stairs.

"Have you left the house today?" I asked, trying not to sound judgy.

He shook his head. "Nope."

"Wanna go out tonight? Go shoot some pool at the Knuckle?"

He shook his head, stopped the game, and tossed the controller onto the sofa. "Nah, got a date. Not taking her there."

I lifted an eyebrow. "With who?"

He stood and stretched, and I noticed he was still in his clothes from yesterday. "I'll tell you if I get a second date. If not, don't worry about it, man."

I also stood and grunted. "I wasn't worried."

He wandered to the staircase, I presumed to shower and get ready.

"Hey, Jalen."

He turned around before his foot hit the top stair. "Yeah?"

"Can I move in?"

He laughed. "It's your house, and of course. You already have. You staying for good?"

I nodded. "Yes, nothing for me back in Colorado Springs."

Jalen smiled, and it was the first time since I returned that he seemed genuinely happy. "You got a job?"

"Yep, remember I told you Gwen hired me at Tragic Ink? Gonna start next week."

"Awesome," my cousin replied as he sprinted up the steps.

I went into the kitchen and wondered what I was gonna do with myself for the rest of the night. I could go to the Dirty Knuckle by myself, but that would be kinda sad. It sucked that none of the friends I grew up with could hang out with me—either they'd left town, or they were in serious relationships. Some were even married.

I turned on the satellite radio console we kept in the kitchen and pushed the button for the classic rock station. As Metallica began to bleed from the speakers, I opened the fridge and pantry to search for shit to cook. As usual, there wasn't much, but I found sauce, noodles, and sausage to make spaghetti. As I sang along and banged my head to "Enter Sandman," I thought about Scottlin. Even though I had just seen her yesterday, I missed being near her. I missed talking to her. She was so sweet, almost innocent-like. She was funny in a subtle way, and I had mad respect for what she did for a living. But I couldn't be mad at her for not wanting me.

As I was browning the sausage over the stove, I clenched and unclenched my hand several times. The people at the hospital had called to say my X-rays looked great, but I still felt weak in my right hand. I supposed it would get better soon as my healing ability kicked in—but it would also take time. At least the cut was gone, thanks to Scottlin's magic.

I dumped noodles into the boiling water and almost dropped the package as I heard Def Leppard begin to croon through the speakers. Reminded immediately of her, I closed my eyes and listened to them belt out "Love Bites."

I had the urge to go over and shut off the damned radio, but I couldn't bring myself to do it. So I did what any fool would do: I opened the music app on my phone and downloaded the song so I could torture myself with it any time of the day or night.

I poured the sauce over my cooked sausage and stirred it around, wishing I had something better to distract myself with. Half relieved and half sad that the song had ended, I blew out a breath and went to the fridge to grab a Coors to go with my spaghetti. Just before I cracked it open, Jalen walked in. He was all cleaned up in jeans and a fitted T-shirt with his wool jacket over it. His hair had goop in it, and he had put on cologne.

"Smells good," he said.

"It's gonna taste even better," I replied.

"See ya," he said, leaving.

I was jealous of him. I leaned my ass against the counter with the beer in my hand. Then an idea hit me.

After turning off all the burners, I grabbed my keys and flew out the door. As the icy wind blasted through my hair, I pushed the throttle on the bike faster so I wouldn't lose my nerve. It seemed I was doing a lot of brave things today.

The sun had set, and the night had taken over. As the day had been a tad warmer than usual, a light rain began to fall, and I was grateful it wasn't snow. As I drove, I looked up at the snowcapped mountains. The moon was full, and heavy clouds drifted through a star-shot sky.

Once I reached Scottlin's apartment complex, I killed the engine to my bike, then walked around to where her apartment was and looked up through raindrops falling into my eyes to see the light on.

The parking lot was so quiet. What I was about to do was risky, but it had to be done. I wasn't here out of boredom; I was here because seeing Scottlin yesterday had stirred things inside me that I thought I had pushed aside. Because I had to try to get her back, no matter the cost.

At the end of the day, I knew I wasn't fooling anyone. I knew there wouldn't ever come a day where I wouldn't miss her or think about her. Because I lacked the nerve to walk into the apartment building and risk having her not open the door like before, I was going to lean on the cheesy, romantic—yet seemingly effective—moves of an old 1980s movie.

I pulled the phone from my pocket and found *Love Bites* on the playlist. After turning the volume on my phone all the way up and plugging it into my Bluetooth speaker, I pushed play and let the song float from it.

With the phone in one hand and the speaker in the other, and happy they were waterproof, I held them high above my head with my face upturned toward her apartment window, the raindrops now turning to freezing rain. The pellets assaulted my face in hard, cold stings.

I didn't care.

Then, for good measure, I even sang along. Loudly and badly.

A couple of dogs barked and howled. A few lights in the complex flipped on, but I paid them no mind. I was anxiously awaiting movement from the curtain in Scottlin's window.

I was starting to shiver, but I persevered, continuing to sing along.

Finally . . . *finally*, I saw the curtain move and a pale face peer out. Our eyes met. Hers went wide, while I just kept singing like a fool.

"Shut up!" a male voice yelled from somewhere. I ignored him.

The curtain on Scottlin's window flicked closed, and it wasn't long until she stormed out the front door of the building, looked around, and yelled, "Karson! What do you think you're doing?"

I continued to sing about not wanting to touch her too much, and how making love to her might make me crazy.

She looked around, the rain quickly soaking her. "Karson!"

I muted the phone, shoved it into my pocket, and set the speaker on a nearby planter, all without breaking eye contact. I stalked hungrily toward her, and when I was within a foot, I looked down into her face, which was quickly becoming streaked with rain.

I sighed. "I miss you, Scottlin."

Her eyes went wide again, and when I reached out and grabbed her face with both hands, she gasped, but did not pull away. I stared deep into her eyes. "I'm sorry. I'm so fucking sorry. I'll do anything for a second chance. Anything. Don't make me grovel, baby. *Please.*"

Without waiting for an answer, I leaned down, pressed my lips to hers, and captured her mouth. She didn't resist at all, but instead put her arms around my neck and kissed me back under the chilly, hard-falling rain.

A few catcalls and whistles could be heard, but we ignored them.

"It's freezing out here," she said. "Come inside."

I didn't have to be told twice. I snatched the speaker from where I'd set it, and she led me by the hand into the warmth of her building. We quickly walked up the stairs together, and as soon as I closed the door to her apartment, she turned around and pierced me with a look I couldn't decipher, water dripping off her nose and chin. Confusion and hope mixed with a little lust was the only way to describe what was going on behind those blindingly beautiful blue eyes of hers.

I walked over to her and put my arms around her. "I'm sorry. A thousand times over, I'm so sorry. Please let me make it up to you."

"It's not me you need to apologize to. It's Len," she replied quietly, untangling herself from me. She used her hand to dry off her face and push her hair away.

"Done. Tell me where to find him, and I'll do it right now," I replied, meaning it.

"I don't know where he is now, but I'm gonna hold you to that."

"You have my word." I could see her hair was out of the braids, and I took a step closer to push some behind her ear so I could look at her face. "I can't do this without you."

She flicked her gaze back and forth between my eyes. "Do what?"

I let out a deep sigh. "I'm getting help for my anger. For the shit from my childhood. Dr. Espensen is great. I'm so glad you gave me her card."

Her eyes went wide. "You already saw her?"

I nodded. "Yep, called the same day. I talked to her this morning."

She smiled, and it was so beautiful. "I'm so glad, Karson, I really am." Her smile then fell. "Because I can't be with someone who can't control their anger. Your temper is gonna be your downfall." She turned around like she was trying to hide emotion.

I couldn't take it any longer. Her cherry-red lips were too tempting, so I touched her shoulder and turned her around. Without asking, I claimed her lips again, just before she gasped in surprise. She melted into me and sighed in pleasure.

With nothing left to be said, I picked her up while I continued to kiss her. I spied the one and only bedroom in the apartment, and I made my way toward it while running kisses along her jaw, cheek, nose, and mouth.

"Karson," she gasped when I set her down on the bed.

I removed my jacket and threw my keys to the floor. "What, beautiful?"

"I don't know—"

I froze. "If you don't want this, just say so now, and I'll leave. But Scottlin . . . just know that I can't stay away from you. You're an addiction I haven't been able to kick. You're like nobody I've ever met, and I think I'm falling in love with you. Please say you feel the same?"

I was damn near breathless now. I'd never wanted anyone so badly in my life, and by the way she sucked her bottom lip between her teeth, and the blue flame of desire burning behind her gaze, I knew she couldn't deny how she felt any more than I could.

Slowly, she nodded. Then she took me by surprise. She rose from the bed, pulled her tee over her head, slid her black pants off, and stood in front of me in nothing but lace panties, milky white skin, and the most beautiful body I had ever laid eyes on.

I wasn't sure I'd ever disrobed as quickly as I did in that moment, but once my clothes were off, I stalked over to her like a hungry animal, picked her up, and kissed her as she wrapped her legs around me.

Once she was under me, we let go of our inhibitions and loved each other for hours upon hours. I showed her how much I'd missed her, and she accepted all I poured into her. I wasn't sure we even slept that night. And if we didn't . . . it was totally worth it.

As I looked down into her sleeping face, I knew in that moment she'd attached herself to my soul. And if she ever stopped looking at me the way I looked at her, it would destroy me. Because there are things worse than death, and not having the love of my life as a part of my forever would be just that.

Scottlin was beautiful, the complete package, and she had wrecked me in the most perfect way possible.

I wouldn't have it any other fucking way.

EPILOGUE

KARSON

FEBRUARY 14

*A*s we all sat eating a nice dinner at the Fallview Tavern, we discussed whether or not we wanted to go to the Cupids & Cuties Valentine's Day event. It was, after all, at Whisper Falls Inn, the owner being Michaela, the daughter of Mihail Petran, whom Uncle Will had stung and almost killed five years ago. He'd passed since then, but not because of what Uncle Will had done. Still, we weren't sure how cool the Petrans were with the Kanes. None of us had attended the event since.

"I think it'll be fine," Scottlin said.

"We'll only have to stay for a little while," Jalen added, before shoving a carnation he'd plucked from the centerpiece on the table into his mouth.

Scottlin made a face. "Did you just . . . eat a flower?"

I chuckled. "They're like a delicacy for us."

"Gives us a little tiny buzz," Dad commented before taking a swig from his beer.

"Um, well, that's interesting," Scottlin said.

Regina chuckled. "I have to watch my flowerbeds around this one." She elbowed her husband in the ribs.

"So what do you think? Think we should go?" I asked. "I have a gift, like a peace offering." I lifted up the small bag containing a bottle of expensive wine that Scottlin had helped me pick out at Sanguine Elixirs—a special blend for vampires.

"Yeah, let's just stay there for an hour and leave. We have to head out to the falls later, anyway," Gavin said.

I smiled. It was good to see him again for his monthly visit.

After a short drive, we arrived at the inn. My arm around Scottlin, we entered the lobby. For the special occasion, I'd forgone the band tee in place of a red button-down shirt and some black slacks. Scottlin wore a deep red dress that reached her feet, and some kind of white furry thing around her shoulders. Her hair was up in some twist thing. She looked stunning.

When we stepped inside, the party was in full swing, as we'd arrived about an hour late. I was a little relieved nobody was handing out those stupid gold-tipped arrows that were supposed to lead you to your "one true love." I'd already found her, and that would have just been fucking awkward.

The ballroom was already crowded with people dancing and standing around, talking with drinks in their hands. Jalen and his date, along with my dad and Regina, all went separately to the bar or to talk to people.

"Want to dance?" I asked my beautiful girlfriend.

"Sure."

As I led her out onto the dance floor, we got a few looks and smiles, but nobody said anything. Over the past month, we'd made no secret of our relationship. I held Scottlin close as we danced, reveling in the feel of how perfectly she fit against me. I didn't fail to notice that Mihail's sister-in-law was hovering in a corner, staring at us.

Scottlin looked up at me. "Why is Madame Luiza staring at us?"

I sighed. "From what I understand, she's all that's left—if you could call it that—of that generation of Petrans. She's a ghost."

"Oh. Awkward. Nothing like having a ghost staring you down."

I chuckled. "Yeah. But I can't wait to see Uncle Will tonight."

She nodded. "You dropping me off first?"

"I'd like you to come," I said hopefully.

She rested her head on my chest. "I'd like that."

Michaela Petran and her boyfriend Xandru Roca greeted us, and they were nothing but friendly and welcoming. It made me feel better. As I looked around at my cousins and Dad, I could see they were a little relieved, too.

After we had all changed out of our party clothes, we stood on a large outcropping of rock, the powerful falls rushing all around us. I held Scottlin's hand firmly in mine. My dad and Regina, along with Jalen and Gavin, stood near the entrance to the falls. This was the day we'd been waiting for. This was why Jalen had wanted me to return to Havenwood Falls.

But had that been the only reason? No, I didn't believe it was. That being said, I didn't think it really mattered anymore. Uncle Will was coming back to us, and this was a very important day.

We all turned to look when a strange light shimmered before our eyes, and from out of it stepped my Uncle Will, hands bound in glowing supernatural bindings and wearing a yellow jumpsuit. His hair was longer than I remembered, and a long, white-gray beard and mustache framed his mouth. He was escorted by two muscular Seelie guards.

A woman I hadn't noticed before came forward, put her hands on my uncle's head, and whispered something. He closed his eyes, and we saw her hands glow yellow. Once he popped his eyes open, he blinked rapidly, looking around.

"I think she's restoring his memories," Scottlin whispered.

When William spotted Jalen and Gavin, his dulling purple eyes went wide, then filled with unshed tears. "My boys," he cried.

Gavin and Jalen tried to rush up to him, but the Seelie guards put their arms out to block them. "Please stand back."

I frowned. My cousins couldn't even embrace their father, whom they hadn't seen in five years?

"It's not right," Scottlin whispered, her warm breath on my ear.

"I agree," I replied.

Uncle Will kept his eyes trained on his sons as the guards passed him off to two Havenwood Falls deputies. After the Seelies disappeared through the portal, which quickly vanished, the deputies put him in an unmarked white van. When they drove away from the falls and toward town, Scottlin and I quickly mounted my bike and followed. The others were right behind us in their cars.

The white van stopped at the sheriff's station, and I respected them enough to park my bike at a distance and stand back as they escorted Uncle Will inside. When Jalen and Gavin got out of the car and went into the jail area, Scottlin and I followed. We knew he had to spend six weeks in Sheriff Kasun's jail, and had accepted that.

Once Uncle Will was uncuffed and then secured in a cell, a deputy spat tobacco into a Styrofoam cup and pierced us with an authoritative stare. "You have ten minutes, elves. Make it count." Without another word, he left the cellblock and disappeared though a door.

My uncle stood gripping the thick bars of his cell, the same one Jalen had been in weeks ago.

"Dad, we've missed you so much," Jalen said, fighting back emotion as he hugged his dad through the hard metal bars.

Gavin hugged him next, followed by Ellis. I gave him a quick one, too.

Will grinned at his sons. "I've missed you so much."

"Good to have you home," my dad said to his brother.

"I need to see him. I need to apologize," Will said, and we knew whom he meant. He sat down on the bed inside the cell.

"He passed away a few years ago," I said.

My uncle looked shocked. "Probably from what happened in court. It wasn't right, what I did."

"No, it wasn't. He was already circling the drain, trust me." Dad said quickly.

Uncle Will nodded, his brow furrowed. I could tell he would never forgive himself.

"Totally sucks you have to stay here," Jalen grumbled.

Will looked up and smirked. "Boy, I can do six weeks standing on my head here compared to where I've just been."

"And where is that?" Gavin asked, crossing his arms over his turquoise polo shirt.

Will looked at his other son. "You don't wanna fuckin' know, kid. Just be here in six weeks when I get out so we can go party at the Knuckle. Then . . . you'll have to get me drunk as fuck if you want me to talk about that place."

Gavin nodded, and I remembered him calling his dad a shitbag. Now that I had my memories back, I knew why—they'd always had an extremely strained relationship. Still, Gavin had shown up here, so that said something.

Uncle Will looked at Scottlin, then drifted his gaze to me. "What you been up to, boy? Still a hothead?"

I glanced down at my beautiful girlfriend, my arm around her delicate shoulders, then back to my uncle. "Nah, not anymore." I kissed Scottlin's nose, then looked at Uncle Will. "Welcome home, asshole."

We hope you enjoyed this story in the Havenwood Falls series featuring a variety of supernatural creatures. The series is a collaborative effort by multiple authors.

Read the book where we first meet Scottlin - *Defying Gravity* by Kallie Ross. You can also read about Addie Beaumont, starting with *Forget You Not* and *Lose You Not*, then continuing with her own story in *Break Me Not*, all by Kristie Cook, as well as *The Collector: Awakening* by Kristie Cook, R.K. Ryals, Belinda Boring & Nadirah Foxx. Read about Karson's cousin Tarron in *Written in the Stars* by Kallie Ross.

Also look for the YA line, Havenwood Falls High; the historical paranormal line, Legends of Havenwood Falls; the sexier side of town, Havenwood Falls Sin & Silk; the local supernatural college, Sun & Moon Academy; and the Havenwood Falls holiday short story anthologies.

Stay up to date at www.HavenwoodFalls.com

ABOUT THE AUTHOR

C.J. is a USA Today bestselling author living in Colorado. Lover of red wine, wearer of fabulous shoes, and die-hard Niner fan, she's also an editor at heart. She's the author of over thirty novels and short stories that contain both contemporary/new adult and paranormal romance that are a little bit badass, a little heart-wrenching, and sorta funny (to her, anyway). Almost all of her books contain law enforcement or military undertones, since strong, brave, alpha men and women are her weaknesses. When she's not writing, she can be found working at a very strange day job, which may or may not have some mild influences on her gripping stories—so strange, in fact, she may just write a book about it one day.

You can find her on Facebook, Instagram, and Twitter, or on her website, www.cjpinard.com

ACKNOWLEDGMENTS

Thank you Heather, Kallie, Kristie, and Michelle for letting me use your amazing characters. Thank you, Liz, for your amazing copyediting skills. And lastly, thank you Kristie for creating this world, and then editing Karson and Scottlin's story so it was perfection for Havenwood Falls.

AN EXCERPT

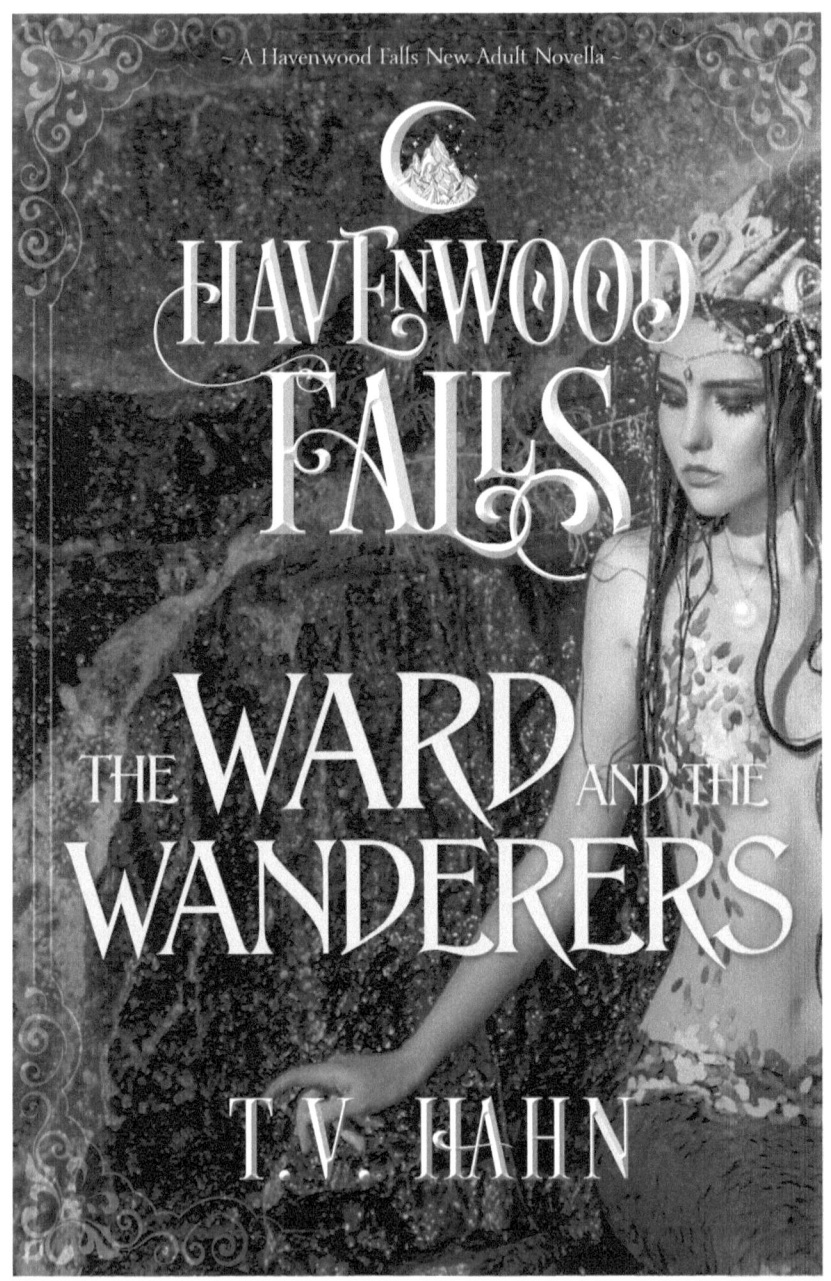

~ A Havenwood Falls New Adult Novella ~

Havenwood Falls

The WARD and the WANDERERS

T.V. HAHN

The Ward & the Wanderers (A Havenwood Falls Novella) by
T.V. Hahn

**In this sequel to *The Winged & the Wicked*, Teeny Weeny is off to
save her little mermaid friend in another Teeny Weeny Fairy Tale.**

Teeny Weeny Tahini's life had always been quiet and simple, just
the way she liked it. At least, until a year and a half ago, when her owl-
shifter nephew Mat came to town with trouble on his heels. She and
her extraordinary friends saved the day, but their happily ever after was
short-lived. Now, the spring faerie has been haunted not only by
nightmares, but also her past.

Compelled to travel thousands of miles to her ancestral home,
Teeny Weeny leaves the safety and security of Havenwood Falls for the
Isle of Gwynf'l, off the coast of England. Coralie, her long-time
mermaid friend, is in danger, and the only way to save her is to take
her back to Havenwood Falls. A series of obstacles combined with
personal dilemmas from Teeny's past make it a foreboding journey, but
one she must endure.

Traveling with a mermaid isn't easy, and the return trip could be
racked with more problems because of the town's protective wards that
only give her a lunar cycle away from her safe haven. Teeny Weeny and
Coralie, not to mention a few uninvited travelers, race against time
before they lose all memories of the place they now call home.

THE WARD & THE WANDERERS

BY T.V. HAHN

"FATHER, NO!"

"Siobhan, stay out of this. Your brother has disobeyed the code, and for that he must be punished."

My mother stood beside my father, crestfallen and bereaved.

Grenfold stood firm, silent, accepting of his fate. If he only knew.

My father chanted the code. "We, this family of fae, are of earth and air. When sea mixes with earth, it becomes mud. When sea mixes with air, tears fall from the heavens. You have brought both to this family. To be true, from this day hence, no longer are you fae, a prince. For your crime I extol, from this day forward, your life, a troll."

With that, King Ian—for he acted as king now, and not as a loving father —waved his royal wand above my brother's head, and the glowing orb at its tip touched my brother's brow. The first sounds Grenfold made since the commencement of this ghastly ceremony— which was unfairly replacing our usual festive Rites of Spring—were of such pain and agony that nothing human could compare to what my once beautiful brother was suffering. I knew this because over the years, as an empath, I had felt human pain, and this was something far beyond it.

The decibels and frequencies of my brother's cries were otherworldly as his body was transformed. The graceful, perfect frame

145

of the handsome prince made a grotesque crunching of bones as his back disintegrated into a warped spine. My brother's cries and the horrific crackling of cartilage rocked the Isle of Gwynf'l to its core. His hands and feet became gnarled and twisted. His gorgeous golden locks fell in clumps from his head to be replaced by a wiry configuration of corkscrew strands, and even those had a resonance that I could taste as acrid and fuzzy on my tongue. His bright hazel eyes became like lumps of coal placed in a bed of gray clay, as his handsome features distorted. His nose became a long crooked probe with crusty warts, and his mouth turned and twisted, totally malformed, filled with protruding and decayed teeth.

After this horrible transformation was complete, my father, the great King Ian, ordered the troll to find a rock to crawl under.

And so he did.

My mother, the kind and generous Queen Rose, was so heartbroken, she turned ill and died within a few short months after Grenfold's departure.

Such is the price one pays for love. It didn't seem right that a gift of love should be so painful, so costly.

The tinkling of the shopkeeper's bell rang sweetly in the dining room of Broastful Brew as I entered and slowly closed the shop door behind me, accidentally allowing a brisk March wind to add a bit of chill to the café. I trudged into the toasty coffee house and made my way to the back table, where my best friend, Barbie Stuart, the mayor of Havenwood Falls, sat sipping a simmering cup of coffee.

Havenwood Falls was no ordinary Colorado town. Oh sure, it looked like your typical frontier Victorian village one could find nestled in just about any canyon in the state, with the sun rays glistening off the golden aspens' fluttering leaves and the scent of pine wafting in the cool breeze. I could assure you, however, that was just a façade. Behind the brick and mortar, wood shingles, and gingerbread lattice work was a town full of supernaturals, from vampires and demons to werewolves and angels. In fact, I was one of them, a spring fae.

Not all of the townsfolk were supernaturals. The ratio varied from time to time, ranging between forty and sixty percent supes. I think it depended on how the stars aligned, but I could be wrong. There could be something much more mysterious behind the mix.

Regardless, the town was founded by the Old Families, one of which was mine. We were—and yes, some of us are still quite alive and kicking—supernaturals looking for a safe haven, where our supernatural abilities would not subject us to prejudice, as we discovered would happen just about anywhere else.

The founders created the town and the government known as the Court of the Sun and the Moon. All of the Old Families had one member sitting on the Court. I held my family's seat, although I was basically the wallflower of the group most of the time.

The Luna Coven created most of the magic that protected Havenwood Falls, including something the town referred to as the "memory ward." As soon as a visitor traveled outside of the twenty-five mile radius of the town's limits, their memory of our little haven vanished. The residents got a bit of a reprieve on this mystic cloak, in that we could exit town for one complete moon phase—twenty-eight days—before our memories of Havenwood Falls disappeared.

I found Havenwood Falls serene and comforting, and really never had any reason to go anywhere outside of its protective borders. Others—a Roca here and a Bishop there—seemed to have a necessity to come and go frequently.

I withdrew the chair from the table when the mayor looked up at me. She was visibly startled at my appearance.

"Siobhan! You look dreadful! Is it the spring equinox that's bothering you? I've never seen you look so . . . well, so bad." Barbara, a dear friend and a member of another Old Family, invited me to join her.

Barbie had listened to me recount my family tale every spring for what seemed like a hundred years, and may very well have been. We met regularly at Broastful Brew. Unlike the bustling Coffee Haven, where the younger folk liked to hang, Mabel's coffee shop was quite sedate and the perfect place for us two to congregate.

Barbie's stature was so starkly different from mine, me being only four foot five, the town's mysterious palm reader and potion mixer, lovingly (I think) known as Madame "Teeny Weeny" Tahini. By contrast, Barbie's six-foot frame was not enough to intimidate, her bouffant beehive hairdo—which she sometimes dyed in various pastel colors according to her whimsy so it looked like a wand of cotton candy—added at least six more inches to her height.

Tahini was not really my surname. It was McFeeny, but being a palm reader and all, I felt Tahini gave it a much more exotic allure for my trade, and it rhymed with McFeeny. For that matter, it rhymed with Teeny Weeny, too.

Normally I was very cheerful and lighthearted, or so I'd been told. Barbie always said I had a childlike nature of wonderment drifting about me. However, this day my faerie glamour wasn't sparkling, dark circles rimmed my eyes, and my generally shiny long brunette hair was in a fizzled mess around my shoulders. I'd noticed the ghastly reflection in the glass door before I entered.

"I haven't been sleeping well, Barbie. I've been bombarded with nightmares. I can't make anything of them. It's just so weird for me. The Rites of Spring dream—I'm used to that. For so long, I've relived that moment, and I have wished I had the power to break my father's curse."

Barbie nodded with understanding, but she raised one eyebrow, as if she thought differently about my wish.

She wrapped her large soft hands around my tiny wringing fists, trying her best to comfort me.

"You poor dear," she said soothingly. "Maybe these nightmares stem from that awful incident with that Pisik cat-shifting witch and your poor nephew Mat. You are not so accustomed to commotion."

I smiled weakly at my friend's attempt at assonance—word play had always been one of my favorite forms of dialogue. But not so much today, or for the last week or so, for that matter.

"Tell me about the nightmare. It might help to talk it out. Maybe between the two of us, we can fathom its meaning," she prodded.

"Well the first one—" I started.

"First one! There's more?"

"Nightmarezzz," I exaggerated wearily, emphasizing the plural, then continued. "The first one starts out in the dead of winter. The snows have already fallen heavily in the canyon. I have effervesced and flown up to Peacock Lake. The triplet falls are frozen solid, and the lake is like a shining mirror. I'm barely able to discern any of its radiant colors. I am enjoying the crisp, fresh smell of the whiteness. The air is so clean, the scent of the pines is outright singing to me at Small's Falls. I am listening to the soft chords of the sunlight passing through the icicles on the falls' ledge, spraying the colors like a prism, a harp strumming angelic psalms across the lake. It's peaceful and serene, and I am enjoying the scenery."

I paused, then continued, "Suddenly, black irregular spots begin to appear across the snowy landscape. They grow bigger, dripping upon the land, as if something black and evil is clawing at the snow-laden mountains. The blackness runs like spilt ink, and the spots begin to run into one another, growing larger. The smell is so acrid, sticky, like the smell of crude oil, but worse, like deeper than those bowels of the earth. It is a smell so strong that I wake up drenched in sweat, unable to shake the odor from my nostrils and way too afraid to try to go back to sleep."

Barbie sat unblinkingly as she pondered the dream's description and sipped her coffee. Mabel had brought my usual pot of hot water and favorite chamomile tea in a bag. I half-heartedly bounced the teabag up and down in the pot, but I was just not really inclined to actually pour the tea into my cup.

"Not sure I can make much of that. *Yet.*" Barbie went on, "Normally, it doesn't sound like much to make such a sweat over— sorry, no pun intended. However, you do have that ultra-synesthesia thing going on. You know, where you *feel* smells so strongly, and *hear* colors so vividly, and a bunch of other mixed up senses, that it's perfectly understandable. Maybe it's connected to the next dream. Tell me about that one?"

There were not too many folks in town who knew the mayor had a talent for interpreting dreams. Maybe it was just her curiosity in netherworldly ways, or maybe an inheritance she had yet to expose.

Barbie was supposedly human, but I had my doubts, having known her for so long. Even with our long friendship, I had just learned some of her secrets at her last Thankshannamas gathering, when she thought she had lost her dragon pendant, a family relic that evidently gave her strength and agelessness when she wore it. I had noticed long before that she never changed, except, of course, for the mound of cotton candy that topped her crown. From time to time, her hair color had been pale blue, pale pink, pale yellow, pale purple, pale whatever, a pastel rainbow of sorts. The pale yellow must've been her favorite, at least when in public, but every now and again, she would get a little adventurous. And each color smelled like . . . well, pale blue like blueberry, pale yellow like lemon chiffon, etc. At least to me, which was yummy.

I remembered when she had it almost a lavender color, but lavender was not the scent I'd picked up. I'd had a hard time identifying it.

"Welch's grape juice," she'd remarked.

That was it! It smelled like grapes. Did she soak that magnificent head of hair in a vat of Welch's grape juice, or was it just her inspiration? I didn't know. Maybe someday she'd tell me.

But like I said, Barbie had never changed—other than the color of her hair—for decades. On the other hand, she had never exhibited any supernatural powers either, in public or to me, other than that ancient talent of dream interpretation. Then again, she did seem to have some superhuman strength, or I could be imagining it. Since she's so much larger than I am, her own human abilities might just be that strong in comparison to me having to use my faerie dust to accomplish something similar, like picking up beings twice my size, as an example.

She'd held so many different positions in town and on the Court, but had always been a major presence. And she was never without the dragon pendant (which most folks thought represented the high school mascot) that hung precariously from a silver chain around her neck, with its tail always pointing to a voluptuous cavern of cleavage, as she was very well-endowed.

As to her requesting me to tell her about the *next* dream, I obliged.

"So the next time, I dreamed I was sipping a delightful cup of tea in front of the blazing fireplace in the parlor of Whisper Falls Inn. Madame Luiza is sitting with me in her ghostly form, and we are having one of our lovely chats about the town's ancient history, and the miscreants that once inhabited our wonderful village, and the few who still do. You remember what it was like? We are having such fun, as Luiza describes so many of the colorful characters and their doings and misdoings. She saw and knew so much. It is always fun talking with her."

Barbie nodded her lemon-chiffon head, recollecting those chats herself, but waved her large beautiful hands in a come-forward gesture, begging me to continue.

So I did.

"The fire in the hearth suddenly crackles loudly, and fiery sparks fly out of the fireplace. We stand up immediately, trying to bat at the tiny sparks that could alight and place the entire inn in peril. Of course, Luiza is a ghost, so her batting is totally useless. A swirl of black smoke emits from the embers and circles throughout the room, thickening the air, making it nearly impossible to breathe. I am grasping at my chest, trying to gasp at least one more ounce of oxygen into my lungs before the horrific smog-like smoke takes over. There is a similarity in the smoky stench and that oily odor from the previous dream. At this point, I wake up, once again dripping with sweat, the pungent smell still burning in my nose and an ominous, dull ringing tone tolling in my ears."

Barbie sympathetically shook her head and patted my hands. "It's interesting that these dreams start out so . . . well, so dreamy. Then they kind of catch you off guard and take a sudden turn. So that's something to keep in mind. It might be that your dreams are foretelling the fortune teller something. Maybe you need to keep your guard up. Seems like you need to be on the alert."

"Yeah, you might be right, because the next one is like that too," I confided.

"Next one? You mean there's even more?" The mayor grimaced, realizing suddenly why I looked so miserable.

"One more, actually."

Barbie's brow raised higher than I thought capable, so I continued.

"I am back on the Isle of Gwynf'l with my parents and my brother, before, well, you know, before Father changed him. It is a beautiful day, and we are having a faerie picnic on the shore by the Bay of Gwynf'l. Mother has baked our favorite faerie cakes of honeysuckle honey and daisy flower flour. The pixies are skipping along the mollusk shells scattered on the beach and breaking out into their familiar wrestling matches in the sand. The waves are bright aqua topped with marshmallowy sea-foam, and they are gently lapping the shore. There are mountainous fluffy clouds in the sky, and they send sound waves of comforting lullabies and happy Irish ditties toward the sandy dunes that buffet the beach.

"I spot a waterspout forming out in the sea, and I am mesmerized by the sight of the swirling funnel, so magnificent in its perfect Fibonacci spiral. The funnel, though, is moving quickly closer and growing darker and larger. It is suddenly totally black as it reaches the shore, and a giant wave crashes over all of us, smelling like . . . Well, like before—oily, inky, black. And I awoke as soaked as if the wave had actually hit me, and this time I began to vomit from the odiferous air that surrounded me."

"This is not good, Siobhan! You should have called me earlier. We will have to be vigilant, since I am sure these are *warning* signs."

"But there's something else, also," Barbie continued. "I don't know if it's the smell or the black thing, maybe both. I will have to think more about this. No matter what, if you have another dream, you are to call me pronto, regardless of what time it is, understood?"

I nodded in acquiescence to Barbie's order, but my hands were still wringing one another and my teacup still remained empty.

"Drink your tea, hon. It'll help calm you. I have to run. I have a meeting at City Hall with a new visitor. I mean it about calling me!"

I shakily tried to pour the steeped tea from the pot into my cup as Barbie bent over to kiss the top of my head. I struggled to wiggle a few fingers in toodle-oo style, but it probably looked like a very disheartened farewell.

I did finish my tea at the Brew, albeit slowly, since my cup rattled every time I tried to lift it from the saucer, and I was fearful I would spill tea all over the place. I thanked Mabel for letting me sit so long, brooding. I guess today, it could be called Brooding Brew.